ELLIOT MABEUSE

A GAME OF Dress-Up

ELLORA'S CAVE
ROMANTICA PUBLISHING

An Ellora's Cave Romantica Publication

www.ellorascave.com

A Game of Dress-Up

ISBN 9781419960574
ALL RIGHTS RESERVED.
A Game of Dress-Up Copyright © 2006 Elliot Mabeuse
Edited by Shannon Combs.
Photography and cover art by Les Byerley.

This book printed in the U.S.A. by Jasmine–Jade Enterprises, LLC.

Electronic book publication November 2006
Trade paperback publication March 2010

A GAME OF DRESS-UP

ജ

Trademarks Acknowledgement

The author acknowledges the trademarked status and trademark owners of the following wordmarks mentioned in this work of fiction:

Lexus: Toyota Motor Sales, U.S.A., Inc.

Palm Pilot: Pirani, Amin

Chapter One

Wednesday night and Vanessa Wallace was dressing up. The house was empty, her mom and sister were at the movies and she was all alone, free to take her time and do it right. She stood in her bedroom in front of the full-length mirror, watching herself and posing as she slowly and deliberately got dressed in her trashiest and most scandalous clothes, the things she kept hidden beneath the bed locked in a suitcase within a suitcase and pushed back into the farthest corner of the room where no one went but her. It was her own special entertainment, a kind of striptease in reverse, and intended for her eyes only.

She stepped into the tiny black thong panties—scandalously sheer, snug and shot with metallic silver threads—pulled them up over her knees, then hooked her thumbs into the waistband and drew them slowly up her long, smooth thighs, purposely avoiding her reflection in the mirror until they were all the way up. She let the panties snap gently into place over her naked sex and ran her fingers over the smooth, slick fabric, then raised her eyes and looked at herself in the mirror. She looked so naughty, so bad. She just had to smile.

Her suitcase sat open on the dresser and she delved in, taking out the items she planned for her game and anything else that caught her eye. All the clothes, the lingerie, the sex toys and rope, the whips and cuffs—all the things she had secretly assembled for her games from anxious shopping trips and cautious forays on the Web—they were all right there before her. Her whole dream world there at her fingertips like the colors on an artist's palette, all the women she might ever secretly want to be, all the shame, excitement and blatant sexuality.

7

She turned around and looked back at herself over her shoulder so she could see the black thong running like an exclamation point between the proud hemispheres of her behind, then turned back, admiring the way the shiny scrap of fabric barely concealed the trimmed puff of pubic hair, giving the panties a sexy, suggestive bulge, like something ripe and waiting. She looked terribly sexy to herself, terribly desirable, and she allowed herself the luxury of running her fingertip down between her legs, imagining it was a lover's hungry touch. The sight of her red fingernail against the black panties was just as arousing as the shivery sensation of touching herself but she quickly took her hand away before she got carried away. There were rules to this game and they had to be obeyed.

She was alone of course. She wasn't going anywhere and she didn't have a date except in her imagination, and that was part of the game too. She studied hard during the week and when she wasn't studying or helping her mother run the house she was working keeping Mr. Taylor's books, so these few hours alone were a precious time for her — a time for a long, leisurely game of dress-up, followed by a brief, fantasy-fueled masturbation. It was a pastime she rarely had time for anymore. Her schedule and grad school left her no time for a social life, and as the only girl in her advanced studies classes she was something of a rarity and almost invisible to the boys she had to compete against. She'd sacrificed everything for the sake of her scholarship and it was even getting hard to find time for make-believe sex. This was all she had.

It wasn't bad. It wasn't the real thing, but then it didn't have all the messiness and complications of a real relationship either. Vanessa had no illusions about her attractiveness. She had a nice body and a pretty enough face, though she found it distressingly plain unless it was adorned with the exaggerated makeup she only wore when she was playing her game. As a student in mechanical engineering she couldn't afford to wear stylish or feminine clothes for fear she wouldn't be taken as seriously as her male counterparts. Jeans and shapeless sweaters were more her style in public, with her hair pulled back and no makeup. But when she was alone like this and the house was empty, she was someone else entirely.

A femme fatale, a vamp, someone who turned all the men's heads, leaving them devastated and panting, or perhaps allowing herself to fall into their clutches when they simply couldn't control themselves any longer. Then they forced her to do the most deliciously wicked things, forcing themselves upon her and taking her violently, overcome by desires they just couldn't control. But in the end they always fell hopelessly in love with her, overcome by her sheer sexual magnetism.

That was her dream world, and if it wasn't real, it was still deliciously satisfying in its own way. She was free to indulge all her fantasies and desires without worrying what anyone thought. Good taste and fashion sense had nothing to do with it. She wanted to dress in the most obscene and suggestive things she could find. After all, the only one she had to please now was herself. This was her fantasy, and she could be whatever she wanted.

She'd already showered and put on her makeup, more extreme than she would ever have worn in public. Her eye shadow and black eyeliner enhanced her clear brown eyes, and her lipstick was so shiny it was almost obscene. Her earrings were outrageous, long shimmery strands of rhinestone that flashed with the least movement of her head and gleamed wickedly against her dark auburn hair. She'd perfumed herself too and even rouged her nipples to make them stand out. She felt deliciously wicked and wanton and it excited her terrifically.

She turned her back to the mirror and slipped on a black mesh and pleather corset, zipping it on backward and then spinning it around so the zipper was in the back where it belonged. She carefully lifted her breasts into the open demi-cups then took a deep breath. She pulled the front laces hard, cinching her waist in so that the corset hugged her tight — tight as a lover's embrace, accentuating the curve of her hips and forcing her breasts up and out—so tight that even her rouged nipples looked redder, as if the blood from her body were being forced into her breasts.

She allowed herself a peek in the mirror. She never thought of herself as beautiful, and her makeup was intentionally heavy and overdone, but that was all right. In her fantasy world, what mattered was expressing her sexuality, the more blatant and obvious the better.

She was getting very excited now, so she started to hurry. She sat on the bed and pulled on her fishnet hose, drawing them slowly up over her legs, watching herself in the mirror as she extended her foot, pointed her toe and teased the stocking up her thigh. She pulled the stay-up elastic high on her legs and smoothed it into place. She loved the way it gripped her leg, only inches from her sex.

The rule of the game was that she wasn't allowed to touch herself until she was completely dressed and had a fantasy scenario clear in her mind, but a little tease didn't really count, and she took a moment to lie on her side and spread her knees, admiring the contrast of the stockings against the pale flesh of her thighs. She ran her nails down the corset, over the smooth skin of her belly, and finally along the moist fabric of her thong, imagining a lover's tongue following the same path. She could almost feel his hot breath on her skin and the trembling urgency of his masculine desire.

Yes, that fantasy was a favorite—simple and direct. Some poor man couldn't control his lusts, and Vanessa was faced with the choice of giving in to his desperate pleas or holding out 'til he couldn't stand it anymore and simple threw her down and took what he wanted by force, perhaps even tying her wrists so that she was helpless to escape.

By force, yes. That was always so exciting. It was probably her favorite.

The panties she had worn for only minutes were already damp from just thinking about it. She was almost done, but not quite, and control and denial were everything now. The final bit of dressing always had to be done without peeking in the mirror, so as to get the final effect all at once. She put on her wickedly high heels, sexy strappy things that made her legs look even longer than they were, and then the dress.

The dress was the final touch, a buttery soft black vinyl number that snapped all the way up the front. She had bought it a size too small and had grown since then, so that it now fit her like a second skin, pushing her breasts in and compressing them into an erupting cleavage, showing every stitch of the lingerie underneath. The dress hugged her so tightly that even the cleavage between her buttocks showed clearly. It encased her in wicked, shiny black.

She finished snapping it up, took a moment to compose herself and shake her hair free, closed her eyes and turned around to face the mirror. Then she opened her eyes.

Oh yes. Perfect! What a wanton! What a delicious tease she was! She looked as if she was about to burst from the dress, her nipples were hard and clearly visible through the vinyl. The corset accentuated the generous thrust of her hips and the shoes made her look even leggier. She posed for herself, cocking her hip provocatively, raising an eyebrow, blowing a kiss with her red lips. *God she looked cheap!* Cheap and hot. Who wouldn't want her?

She could just picture herself walking into some bar or nightclub—all the men's and even the women's heads turning to look at her. She could imagine the men getting hard in their pants, all that male attention focused on her like a spotlight, the resigned and envious looks of their dates. But no, the women forgave her. They knew she couldn't help it. It wasn't Vanessa's fault she was born to be a sexual siren, cursed to have men lusting after her, and in her heart she knew she was sweetly innocent, a victim of her natural endowments.

The next step in the game was to bring the fantasy scenario to life, to act it out, using her own hands and her secret collection of toys to act the part of her lover, and then, when she was in an agony of arousal, end it with a savage and glorious full-throttle masturbation, the imaginary culmination of her dream lover's terrible desires. But she felt so wonderfully sexy now she didn't want to rush through it. She liked the way her bottom swayed as she strolled in front of the mirror in the heels. She loved the way the dress held her. She cocked her head and watched the earrings sparkle as they kissed her neck. She could feel her own wetness and that only excited her further.

In her mind, the scenario was fairly simple this time. This was her place and she had a man over, just some friend, some good-looking man, maybe the powerful and handsome president of some company she worked for. He'd never seen her like this—never imagined that the staid and hardworking girl he knew at the office was so devastatingly desirable away from her desk—and he couldn't keep his hands off her. He'd seduce her—be helpless to resist—begging her forgiveness even as he whispered the most obscene things in her ear and played his hands feverishly over her body. And Vanessa would protest that he really must control himself. After all, she always dressed like this at home. This was who she was.

She had a sudden urge to have a drink. She didn't like to drink, but she knew she'd have a drink with her boss in the fantasy, and she wanted the liquor as a prop—sophisticated and decadent. Maybe she'd have a cigarette too. She didn't smoke, but she had an old pack she'd bought months ago for another game and she dug the pack out now from among her collection of toys and clothes and put one between her lips. Perfect. She felt terribly European and dissolute.

She walked down the stairs to the kitchen, swaying slightly on the absurdly high heels, and after digging around in some cabinets, found an old bottle of whiskey from God knows when. She put some ice cubes into a glass and poured the whiskey in. She found a book of matches in her mom's junk drawer and lit her cigarette. She took a deep drag into her mouth and blew it out, wondering again why anyone bothered to smoke, then lounged against the sink and sipped the drink.

It was awful. Just terrible, but she forced herself to take a little more. She'd never been able to drink hard liquor but despite the taste, she liked the way it made her mouth feel, the way it stung her throat with just a hint of suppressed evil. Yes, this was what she'd feel like as a vamp, the liquor burning into her and joining with the heat deep inside.

She took another drag and turned to see her reflection in the dark window glass. Her very red lips parted sensuously as she let the smoke trail from her nostrils, then she puckered her lips and blew, just the way she'd blow smoke in some stud's face as a way of telling him to get lost. The gesture was so wicked she felt her nipples harden and she thrust her shoulders back to make her breasts stand out even more. She felt positively lethal.

She raised the cigarette to her lips and inhaled this time, concentrating on not coughing, then turned around and blew a stream of smoke at the light fixture. The nicotine rush made her slightly dizzy, and she leaned her behind against the sink and took another drink.

She was startled by a quick, casual knock on the front door, and before she could even think to react, the door opened and Rob Taylor — Vanessa's boss and a family acquaintance — walked into the room carrying a box of papers.

Vanessa stared at him in shock. There'd been no classes today and she'd totally forgotten this was Wednesday, the day she was supposed to go over and help with his bookkeeping. As he always did whenever she couldn't make it because of her schedule or other conflicts, he had simply brought the accounts over to her house. And now here she was dressed like an absolute tramp, smoking and drinking in her mother's kitchen.

He stared at her and she stared back, horrified.

He looked at her. He looked at the bottle of whiskey. He looked at the cigarette. "Vanessa? What in the world's going on here?"

"Oh my gosh! Mr. Taylor! I'm so sorry. I forgot you were coming!"

He stepped into the room, the look in his eyes changing gradually from shock to lusty appreciation as he took her all in, the shoes, the stockings, the obscenely tight dress. Vanessa looked frantically around the familiar kitchen, as if she could find a place to hide.

"What *is* this, Vanessa?" he asked her. "You going out? Am I interrupting something?"

"No…no. I was just trying on some clothes. I…"

"Is there someone here?" He peered into the living room where the family usually sat, then looked back at her. "Your mother know what you're doing? Has she seen you in this outfit? You think she'd approve?"

"Oh Mr. Taylor. I'm sorry. No, no one's here. I just forgot this was Wednesday and—"

He stepped closer and picked up the bottle of whiskey. "Drinking too, huh? Does your mother know you smoke?"

"No, really, I was just fooling around," she said hurriedly. "Here, let me take the books…"

"No, no, that's okay." He pulled them back as Vanessa reached for them, almost stumbling in her heels. He looked at her again—leered, really. "I'll put them on the desk in the other room."

He walked past her and into the den. Vanessa quickly threw the whiskey down the sink and ran water over the incriminating cigarette then threw it in the trash. She stood nervously by the sink as he came back in and paused in the doorway. She couldn't think of anything else to do.

Rob Taylor was a powerful and attractive man and Vanessa had always had something of a crush on him, which only made her present predicament worse and more humiliating. He'd been a godsend to Vanessa and her mother after her father's death, and it was Mr. Taylor who'd arranged for her scholarship and given her the job that allowed her the flexibility to attend college. Because he dressed well and often worked closely with his clients in his beauty shop and supply business, there were rumors that he was perhaps a touch gay, rumors supported by his separation from his wife, but Vanessa knew otherwise. She'd heard the girls talking and knew that he was a man of some unusual and tantalizing sexual talents, but just what they were she never knew.

In any case, whatever the rumors said there was no mistaking the look in his eye now, a look of undisguised male lust, tempered with a bit of professional appraisal. Rob Taylor wasn't just a hair dresser and businessman, he was a fashion expert, an artist with a woman's face and looks. He'd been a photographer in the past and still did special makeup and consulting jobs for fashion clients in his upstairs studio. His shop was decorated with photos of his work.

"So look at you," he said, leaning against the door jamb. He smiled slowly. "Just look at you."

She didn't know what else to say so she tried to smile, waiting for him to leave. She was mortified and she really didn't want to try to explain herself any further, which would only make things worse. She just wanted him to walk out the door so she could run to her room, get out of those clothes, shove everything back under her bed and pull the covers up over her head and die.

But he seemed to like what he was seeing, or was at least interested.

"Your makeup's terrible, you know," he said.

"Mr. Taylor, really," she pleaded. "It was a game. A game of dress-up."

"I told you before that if you ever wanted me to do you at the shop, it would be my pleasure, Vanessa. You've got a beautiful face. You should know how to use it."

Vanessa quailed. She reached up to wipe the makeup from her face but he stepped forward and took her wrist, holding her at arm's length while he continued to appraise her.

"I didn't even know you had a boyfriend," he said, looking her up and down. "Who's the lucky guy?"

"No, really, Mr. Taylor. There isn't any boyfriend."

"A woman wouldn't dress like that except to please a man," he said. "So you're just going out alone? Dressed like that? I never would have guessed it, Vanessa, a good little girl like you."

For a moment he looked slightly disapproving, as though his parental instinct had kicked in and he thought she should be sent to her room. That look quickly gave way to his previous lecherous stare, and it was clear he didn't want to send her away. "You look like a regular little tramp, you know that? Some hot little piece of tail."

"Oh God, no, I would never let anyone see me like this. No…" she said again, and she twisted her body around in an attempt to get her arm away from him. The snaps on the dress were down far enough to give him a generous shot of her cleavage, which was only enhanced by her twisting and straining, and she could see her own flesh tremble as she fought for her arm.

"But you dress the part," he said. "Is this who you want to be? Is this the real Vanessa? The one we never get to see? Can you back up what the clothes say?"

"Please…"

"Please what, Vanessa? Please what?"

His voice had gotten deeper now, and Vanessa knew something was going to happen that was beyond her control. He grabbed her other wrist and held her, looking her up and down, and they both suddenly realized that they were alone in an empty house, a virile man holding the wrists of a nubile young girl dressed for sex. She'd known Mr. Taylor for almost a year, and he'd always been polite and friendly toward her and supportive of her in her loss of her father. But things had changed now, and as he held her wrists she felt more naked

16

and exposed than if she'd worn nothing at all. Everything she had on said one thing and one thing only.

"You've matured haven't you, Vanessa? And I hadn't even noticed."

He pushed her back, pressing her up against the refrigerator and scattering papers and little alphabet magnets to the floor. He pushed her hands up against her head, holding them there and leaning his body against hers. He was strong and the hardness of his body against her was suddenly unaccountably exciting.

"Mr. Taylor, don't do this," she begged. She tried to remain in control of herself, to calm her breathing and slow her heart, but the feel of his body against hers was doing things to her and making rational thought impossible.

"Don't do what? You think I'm going to let you go out and walk the streets looking like that? You little tramp, your mama will thank me for keeping you in! Do you have any idea how much trouble you could get into? Or is that the whole idea? How long has this been going on, Vanessa? Hmm? How long have you been playing this game?"

"Really, I was just dressing up. Just trying on clothes..."

"Oh sure," he said. "With that makeup and those stockings and heels. And who tries on a vinyl dress like that? Where you going to wear that? To class? Don't bullshit me, Vanessa. There's only one reason a girl gets dressed up like that, and that's to go out whoring. You're going out looking for it, aren't you? You wait 'til your mom's away and then you get all dressed up and go out and find yourself some nice hard cock, don't you, sweetie? Well, you know what?" he sneered. "There's no need to go out looking for it."

Vanessa tried one last time to escape, but Mr. Taylor was just too strong. He took both of her wrists in one hand and pressed her against the fridge with his weight. He used his other hand to slowly draw one finger down her body from her throat to where the last snap strained to keep her dress in place. Then he reached up under the dress and his fingers touched her naked thighs.

"You're all grown up," he said. "You're not some little girl dressing in big girl clothes. You're beautiful, Vanessa, and you know exactly what you're doing, don't you? You should be glad I found you instead of some creep. You should be mighty glad."

"Oh God!" she said in horror, but to Mr. Taylor it sounded like the first sign of arousal, and he pressed himself tighter against her. She closed her eyes and willed the earth to swallow her and her shame, but he was still there when she opened them again, his eyes boring into her, hot with lust.

Vanessa was trembling with fear and humiliation, yet still at a high level of excitement from her game of dress-up, burning with a dizzying mixture of shame and arousal and fear and desire, and the feel of his hard body was wonderful against hers, the one element her game could never supply. Despite her horror and shame, it was just what she wanted to feel, his hardness against her, his strength holding her. She was torn, part of her dying to see her fantasies realized, and part of her ashamed that she would ever let a man take advantage of her like this, ever see her secret desires.

"Come on, Vanessa!" he whispered to her face. "Let's see if you're as hot as you think you are. Let's see just what you've got."

His fingers touched her through her panties and she gasped. Her knees went weak. "Mr. Taylor, please!"

"Jesus Christ!" he swore softly, his forehead almost touching hers. "You're soaking wet! I can feel you through your panties! What the hell have you been doing to yourself?"

"No, no!" she said, but now it was more like a whine. All the force was gone from her voice, all the resistance was fading from her body. She turned her head to the side so he wouldn't see her humiliation and desire, but his fingers slid through the leg band of her panties and touched her naked sex, and a thrill coursed through her like an electric shock, washing away all her strength. Her body didn't want him to stop, and her hips thrust themselves against his hand with a mind of their own as she pressed herself against his seeking fingers.

"You are one hot little piece, Vanessa. All wet and ready to go!"

His lips were right next to hers now, and when he kissed her she couldn't escape—she just closed her eyes and let him do what he wished, whimpered into his mouth in one final, futile plea. He broke away and looked down at her breasts, pushed up and out by the position of her arms above her head, and she saw the hungry gleam in his eye. The thought that her body turned him on so much gave her a strange, fierce thrill, and when his lips came down on hers again, she met his kiss with a hunger and urgency of her own, opening her mouth to let him in.

This had always been her fantasy, to be taken by a man who knew just what he wanted to do with her, and now it was happening, it was every bit as exciting as it was in her dreams. Mr. Taylor was much older than she and far more experienced, and he knew just how to touch her to make her yearn and melt for him. The fact that he was her mother's age was supposed to turn her off, but Vanessa couldn't seem to make her body care.

He slid his hand down the front of her panties, cupping her mound in his hand. He curved his fingers beneath her and found her sex open and ready. He slid the tip of his finger into her and Vanessa stuck her tongue obsequiously into his mouth, imitating what his finger was already doing below. Without thinking she spread her thighs to give him better access, an action that shocked her so much that she moaned in shame at her own behavior. He still held her hands over her head, and his chest flattened her breasts and rubbed against her nipples as they kissed, but it was his hand between her legs that wouldn't let her think straight. To be touched there and violated was so wrong and yet so obscenely thrilling. It just felt so incredibly good and evil at the same time that her

19

hips began to automatically lift toward him in a lewd imitation of the sex she so badly wanted.

"Jesus Christ, you little minx!" he said as he broke the kiss. Vanessa's body humped shamelessly against him, out of control now. "You really need it, don't you? You're lucky I came along when I did, before some stupid kid got his hands on you, Vanessa. You're too good for that. You need to get fucked by a man who knows what he's doing, who can fill that little pussy with some good, hard cock and show you what it's all about."

"No, Mr. Taylor! Please! Don't talk like that! I can't!"

"Can't what, Vanessa? Can't take my hard cock inside you? Can't give me exactly what I want? You're going to get fucked tonight, darling. That much is for sure. Now we can do it sweet and easy or we can do it rough, but you're going down tonight."

He kissed her again, overcome with lust, and his fingers began to pump in and out of her, driving her wild. She already felt loose and lewd and terribly wanton, and now he was confirming it for her, treating her just the way she wanted to be treated, fingering her against her mother's refrigerator in her own kitchen. Of course, she couldn't admit that this was what she wanted. She would never admit she was that kind of girl, but her body didn't lie. She was a molten puddle of need between her legs, and her breasts felt as if they'd explode if he didn't get his rough teeth and lips on them. She was ready to be devoured.

"Please," she said as he licked and bit at her aching mounds, "I'm not like this! I'm not like you think! It was just a game I was playing."

But he wasn't listening to her now and even she was aware of how weak and silly her words sounded. Her body was doing things far truer than anything that was coming from her mouth, and even she didn't believe her excuses anymore. She was lost.

"Come on," he said, stepping back and grabbing her wrist. "Show me where your bedroom is."

She couldn't think straight and she didn't know how to tell him no. Her heart was pounding and her body throbbing with need. She led him dizzily up the stairs, her heels clicking on the hardwood floor, and into her bedroom, forgetting that her sex toys were spread out there among her souvenir pillows and stuffed animals.

He looked at the ropes and vibrators, her handcuffs and whips—all the things she'd purchased so discreetly through mail-order on the internet—and gave her an evil and knowing smile. "Looks like you were going to make a night of it, huh, Vanessa? You like it kinky too, huh? A little bondage? A girl after my own heart."

She stood there dazed, breathless, running her hand through her hair, looking at the toys she had left on the bed. There was no question of what he'd think of her now—she'd never convince him that she was anything but a slut. But for now she didn't care about that. She just wanted to feel his body against hers again, wanted to feel him take her before she came to her senses.

"We can use this," he said, picking up a length of rope. "Turn around."

She turned around automatically, knowing that he'd tie her and wanting to be bound so that she'd have no choice in the matter. Mr. Taylor quickly lashed her wrists together, then spun her back and caught her in a deep and passionate kiss, driving all rational thought from her mind. The helpless feeling of her hands pinioned behind her back flooded her with wild desire to be taken, and she moaned shamelessly as his tongue explored her mouth. His hands came up and he grabbed her breasts right through the dress, squeezing and kneading them, rubbing his thumbs over her aching nipples. Everything he did thrilled her. This was just what she'd wanted, just what she'd dreamed of in her secret fantasies, and now the dream was real.

"If you're going to dress like a tramp, then you're going to show me what a good little tramp you can be!" he said to her as he mauled her breasts and pinched her nipples through the vinyl. "You're going to show me what a good little tramp you are, or I'm going to have a discussion with your mother about how you spend your free time, understand?"

"Oh Mr. Taylor! Mr. Taylor I —"

He stepped back from her, took the lapels of her dress in his hand and pulled them apart, popping the snaps one by one all the way down, exposing her body in the mesh corset to his gaze. Vanessa stood there watching his eyes as he took in her nearly naked body, and what she saw there made her groan out loud — the naked lust, the heated desire and raw excitement. It thrilled her to think that she could inspire such passion in a man. He didn't see an overworked and lonely college student when he looked at her, he saw a hot, desirable woman, and the mere sight of her made his cock hard.

"You sweet little thing!" he said. "What a body! Baby, I could fuck you all night long and not get tired." He grabbed her breasts and began to suck them hungrily, going from one to the other, swirling his tongue around her nipples and biting them softly, making Vanessa's head swim.

She knew she should fight, she should resist him, but her hands were tied behind her back — what chance did she have? Taylor sucked and bit her breasts and Vanessa pulled at her bonds, loving the fact that they held her, loving her helplessness. There was nothing she could do now. It was out of her hands. It was all him now — whatever he wanted to do.

He took her arm and pushed her down onto her bed so that she was flat on her back. Her mind cleared suddenly and she realized what was going to happen — that he was really going to fuck her, put his cock in her pussy and fuck her on her own bed.

She made one last attempt to regain control of herself. "No," she said, "Please! Mr. Taylor, don't do this!"

He was stepping out of his pants and pulling his shorts down, and she saw his cock, big and hard for her, eager for her body. She should have been horrified but the sight excited her tremendously. She wanted that monster inside her. She wanted to feel this older man's weight on top of her, slamming his body into hers, taking her like a woman.

He stepped over to the bed and took his cock in one hand and the back of her head in the other. "Come on, baby!" he said. "Suck me! You know how to do it! Suck my cock, Vanessa!"

She wanted to tell him that she didn't know how. She'd done it to some boys her own age, but he was a full-grown man and she had no real skill, no real experience. But it all happened so fast. Her mouth just opened and he pushed himself inside. She closed her eyes and tasted him, salty and pungent on her tongue, pulsing with a savage life and urgency.

She was so ashamed. She wanted to tell him that she wasn't like this, she wasn't what he thought, but every time she tried to draw off his cock to speak he pushed it back into her mouth. And for all her inexperience, whatever she was doing was making him groan with lewd pleasure and pump himself in and out of her mouth with growing speed.

He pulled her panties off her and threw them aside, and as she sucked his cock he jammed a finger back inside her. She couldn't help it—she spread her legs and he began to fuck her with his finger. She could hear the sloppy sound of his fingers in her wet pussy and it felt so good, but there was more to it than that. It was just so terribly dirty, so obscene to be finger-fucked while she sucked his cock. Her head filled with all sorts of filthy images, with her in the middle of them.

Then he pulled his cock from her mouth. She swallowed and tried to catch her breath. "Mr. Taylor," she whined. "Mr. Taylor…" But for the first time she didn't know what she wanted to say. It wasn't "stop".

She felt the bed sag as he climbed between her legs and got on his knees, and she looked up to see him aiming his big shaft right at the juncture between her thighs. As soon as she felt him make contact with the outside of her labia, she gasped.

"Yeah?" he challenged her. "You don't want this? You don't want my cock in you? Then tell me to stop, Vanessa. Tell me you don't want my big cock inside you reaming you out! Tell me no! Go ahead!"

She knew she had to stop him, that she had to tell him to get dressed and leave her alone, but she just couldn't. She couldn't say anything at all. His cock felt so good pushing against her and spreading her apart, almost inside her. She could feel it throbbing, ready to plunge deep inside. She felt deliciously helpless, at his mercy, just like in her fantasies. She couldn't fight it—she wanted him, wanted him badly.

He smiled at her inability to answer and she felt the thrilling sting of his contempt, then he pushed into her, stretching her open and filling her with his incredible hot, virile hardness, and she groaned at her body's reluctant surrender. Taylor snarled like an animal as he bottomed out at last in her tight sheath, as deep as he could go. He levered himself up on his hands and looked down to where she was stretched around his invading member, and without giving her a moment to adjust he began to fuck her, hard and deep, already almost out of control.

"Yes, Vanessa, yes! Is this good enough for you? You like it like this? Hard like this?"

She couldn't speak, it just felt so good, so right, and his savagery was just what she wanted. She was tired of fighting, not only against him but against her own fantasies as well. She wrapped her legs around him and pulled him tight. Her trapped fingers clawed at the bedspread beneath her as she pushed her breasts up for him to plunder and abuse, and all the while her hips were moving with him, up and down on his stiff pole, sending pangs of raw pleasure through her feverish body.

It had been so long since she'd had real sex with anyone, and never like this, never as she'd dreamed it might be—tied and taken by a man who wouldn't let her escape, wouldn't listen to her excuses. He was driven by his lust for her, and what could she do but let him take her like this, let him use her body for his own pleasure?

"That's my little girl!" he hissed at her as she raised her hips to him again and again. "Now you're fucking like you mean it! You do love it, don't you, Vanessa? Admit it. You love what I'm doing to you!"

"Oh God, yes!" she spit the words out from between clenched teeth. "Yes, I love it! I love it! Do whatever you want with me, just fuck me! Fuck me!"

Her words inflamed him and he pounded into her with renewed fury. This was her bed, her childhood bed. Her collection of stuffed animals was crushed between her and the wall as she writhed against him, her hands pinned beneath her. It just added to her excitement, as if her childhood friends were forced to witness her own humiliation, the corruption of their sweet and innocent playmate.

He groaned above her. "You sweet thing! You're gonna make me come, Vanessa! I'm gonna come in you, baby. Are you safe, Vanessa? Tell me, are you safe?"

She couldn't control her excitement anymore.

"Yes, I'm safe! Do it to me! I want it!" she cried out as he bucked on top of her, making her breasts shake. "I want your hot come! I want all of it!"

Again and again he beat into her, the slick sound of his hard shaft pumping in and out of her wet pussy loud in her ears, along with the frantic creak of the bedsprings, the banging of the headboard against the wall.

"Oh fuck!" he moaned, "oh Christ! Oh Jesus Christ!"

His body went suddenly stiff, ramming her deep, and she screamed as she felt his fingers claw into her breasts. She was crammed with his thickness, and she felt him throb hard and knew that he was shooting his semen into her, filling her with his hot passion.

Her head spun with the erotic nastiness of it. She cried out, and then she came too, thrusting her hips up at him in a spasm of heavenly release as he moaned on top of her. She arched her back and her bound hands clawed the bedspread as she trembled beneath him, the blood roaring in her ears.

She never wanted to come down from that orgasmic high, never wanted to open her eyes again. How could she ever face the shame, the humiliation of letting her boss reduce her to this submissive state, begging him for anything he wanted to give her.

Maybe Mr. Taylor knew her shame, or maybe he was ashamed too because he didn't say a word as he slowly withdrew from her aching body. Still panting, he climbed off her, rolled her onto her side and untied her wrists as if setting a wild animal free. Vanessa felt the ropes slide from her skin but left her hands where they were, as if afraid to reclaim responsibility for them.

She lay there, unable to move, her humiliation warring with a feeling of deep sexual satisfaction like she'd never known. She'd never come like that before—so deeply, so thoroughly, with every part of herself. It had been an orgasm that involved all of her, body and soul, and she didn't know what to make of it or what to make of herself now. Was this truly who she was?

Mr. Taylor was staring at her as he slowly caught his breath. He reached out and ran a hand appreciatively over her trembling body.

"It's not just a game, is it, Vanessa?" he asked her softly. "It goes way beyond that, doesn't it?"

His words confused her and she didn't say anything. She was too ashamed, too utterly humiliated.

He got up and started dressing, stepping into his shorts and pulling on his pants.

26

"You won't believe this, but I understand," he said. "The clothes, the game, the whole thing. I understand perfectly, Vanessa, maybe better even than you do."

She shook her head. "I don't know what you're talking about."

She couldn't see him but she could feel him looking at her, appraising her as he so often did at work, his eyes indulgent and understanding. He sighed, sat down on the edge of the bed and started putting on his socks and shoes.

"No?" he asked. "You don't think I know what you feel when you get dressed like that, or when you put on that kind of makeup? You think you're the only one in the world who dresses up for herself? You think this is just some private game?"

She felt the bed move as he stood up and put on his shirt and started buttoning it.

"I'm in the business, Vanessa. This is what I do. I give women identities they can slip on and off—new faces, new looks, new personalities. You know what we do down at the shop."

He laughed. "Believe me, I know all about it, and I understand. I know what I'm talking about and I understand."

"Are you going to tell my mother?" she asked, alarmed at how small her voice sounded, and how frightened.

He sat down on the bed again and looked at her, his eyes strangely kind and curious.

"Of course not. Vanessa, you're a grown woman. Just because you live in her house and go to school doesn't mean you're a child."

"I'd die if she found out," Vanessa said. "She doesn't know anything about this, about who I really am."

"Who you really are?" he mocked. He laughed. "No one knows who they 'really are'. I won't tell your mother and you don't mention it either and she'll never know. I promise. Okay?"

She nodded in relief, not knowing what else to do.

"Good," he said, standing up. "Then we have an understanding. And I'd better get going before she gets back."

He went to the door then turned and watched her for a while as she lay on her bed. He could see the tears as they squeezed out between her eyelashes even though she tried with all her might to hide them.

He looked at her and his eyes softened. "Why are you crying?" he asked. "Is it because of me? Or because of you?"

"I don't know," she said, holding back the tears. "I don't know what you're talking about. I don't understand any of this."

He walked back over to her, bent over and kissed her on the cheek. "You just had the best orgasm you've ever had in your life, didn't you, Vanessa? And now you're ashamed and horrified. You're ashamed now because of what you did and what you felt, and you think that makes you something bad. You think that says something bad about you."

Vanessa finally broke down. The excitement, the emotion and the shame were just too much for her. "I liked it," she sobbed. "I loved it! I'm not a woman. I'm a slut!"

Her face was in the pillow so she couldn't see how he looked at her—the look of concern and hurt, and then anger. He sat down next to her and reached out and stroked her hair, then put his hand on her shoulder to comfort her, but the contact between them was still so charged with sensual electricity that he quickly removed it, as if she were hot.

"You're still young, Vanessa," he said, and he got up and walked to the door. He stopped and looked back. "Woman? Slut? Those are words. You're more than those, darling. Way more than either. That's what you have to know. That's what you have to remember."

And then she heard him turn and walk slowly down the stairs. She heard him cross the kitchen, heard the door open and close, and she turned her face into the pillow and wept.

Chapter Two

❧

Vanessa stayed away from Mr. Taylor for the next few days, going to classes but avoiding the shop. She was obsessed with memories of their encounter. Filled with feelings of shame and guilt, but they were also accompanied by the most disconcerting feelings of excitement and arousal. She remembered the look of raging lust in his eyes, the feel of his greedy hands on her body and the savage way he'd battered and used her for his pleasure. She tried being outraged and angry, and yet she couldn't escape the conclusion that she'd invited it. She couldn't deny that he'd somehow given her just what she'd wanted, what she'd been asking for, at least in her fantasies. She realized that her anger wasn't directed at Rob Taylor as much as it was at herself, at what she was afraid she might be, way down deep.

She remembered the look in his eyes as they wandered up and down her body stuffed into that skintight latex dress. She had never seen a man look at her that way, though it was what she fantasized about constantly. Or she recalled the hard, almost painful way he'd grabbed her breasts and squeezed them, the way he'd shoved himself into her, so rough and uncaring, as if her body was his to do with what he pleased. She remembered her delicious helplessness, the way it felt like it wasn't her fault. That was part of it too, she knew, and it thrilled her. It thrilled her shamefully.

She'd think about these things as she squeezed a towel between her legs and sought to relive the overwhelming pleasure of that night with her own fingers, but she couldn't. She needed him as a lover and as a witness to who she'd really been that night—the woman of her dreams, the one who drove men mad with desire beyond their ability to control.

29

And yet these feelings were tinged with a terrible fear about seeing Mr. Taylor again. She couldn't put off going into his shop forever, and she was too proud to just quit, and it would be inevitable that she'd see him again. What would he think of her now? How would he treat her? Would other people know what had happened?

She put it off as long as she could, but finally on Friday she simply had to show up. She would go in there in her scruffiest, most unflattering clothes. As far as she was concerned, what had happened was an aberration, a mistake, and she would show him that the person he'd seen that night didn't really exist. Denial seemed to be the best way to deal with it.

She wore a pair of old jeans and a washed-out flannel shirt. She pulled her hair straight back and scrubbed away all traces of makeup. She wore no jewelry. By the time she walked into his shop just as the Friday rush was dying down, she realized she'd perhaps gone too far. The girls looked at her in surprise and someone asked if she was okay. Isabella teased her, "Vanessa? You look like you've come in for a shave! What happened to you, doll?"

Maybe she had gone too far. Maybe one extreme was as bad as another. Vanessa quickly trotted upstairs to the warehouse-studio part of the business where the office was. Taylor's business comprised a salon downstairs, and a large upstairs that served as a warehouse for his beauty supply business and studio for his special makeup jobs. Thankfully, he was working with someone now out on the floor—some art director or designer probably, as there was a rack of new dresses nearby and Taylor was going over color charts. Vanessa was able to slip into the office, put down her school books and go right to work on his accounts.

She was just tallying up the girls' hours when she heard him walk by and stop in the doorway. She knew he was looking at her, and she cursed herself for blushing, but then someone called and he turned and walked off.

The work was easy, but she found herself distracted, making it take much longer than usual as it grew dark outside and one by one the girls brought their receipts upstairs and said good night and the men in the warehouse closed down and locked up. She was aware of how slowly she was working but she told herself that she didn't want to make any mistakes that might belie what had happened. She was doubly aware when she found herself actually totaling up the girls' tips for tax purposes, which was silly, because the girls always reported the minimum amount possible, a mere formality. But still she worked, entering the numbers, adding up the figures, checking and double checking, 'til at last the place was almost empty and Mr. Taylor came in. She took a deep breath but didn't look up from her books. She felt the skin on her neck prickle.

He walked in, leaned against the table on the other side of the room and folded his arms contritely. "Vanessa, I owe you a deep, deep apology. More than an apology. My behavior the other night was inexcusable."

Vanessa felt ice in her veins. Of all the responses she thought she might get, she hadn't expected an apology, and it felt all wrong. He was robbing her of her anger, her main weapon against him.

She said nothing. She put down her pen and sat there, her ears burning. She knew she was blushing.

"You must hate me now, I suppose, and I understand. If you want to leave your job, I'll understand, and I want you to know that I'll continue to support your schoolwork and—"

"No, Mr. Taylor," she said. "I think we should just forget about it. Please. I think that would be the best. It happened. I think we're both sorry. Let's just forget it."

He continued to look at her, and Vanessa couldn't help but remember what she'd looked like the other night, what she'd felt like in those clothes. She could almost feel the tight compression of the latex corset on her as she sat there, and she felt her pulse begin to race.

Mr. Taylor sighed and shook his head ruefully. "You know, it was just such a shock to me when I saw you like that—"

"Mr. Taylor! Please!" She stood up and took some papers to the filing cabinet then realized she had the wrong papers for the wrong cabinet. She stood there, feeling stupid, feeling exposed.

"No," he said. "Let me finish. Seeing you like that. Made up, dressed up. You're a beautiful woman, Vanessa. I've told you that hundreds of times. You could be doing modeling. You don't have to be working in this office."

She kept her head down but her words were tinged with anger. "I'm not beautiful. I'm plain. I have nice skin and my hair can be nice but I'm not beautiful. And I'm not built like those models, all skin and bones. I know very well what I am, Mr. Taylor. I want to be an engineer, not a model."

"Well, forgive me," he said, "but I've been in this business longer than you, at least give me that much. I know a face when I see one, a face that can be made into anything. As for your body, well, there's more to modeling than just couture. Chain stores, ready-to-wear..."

"Mr. Taylor..." she turned to him, and the anger she felt left her. Her words deserted her.

She was looking at the man she'd had sex with the other night, whose cock she'd sucked, who'd devastated her with pleasure, and in his eyes she saw a reflection of the same look she'd seen that night, a look of male lust and appreciation that made her melt inside—the kind of look she always dreamed about.

Something went through them then—some understanding or realization—some brief moment of complete honesty, eye to eye and body to body, and they both felt it.

"Models are easy to find," he said. "Every girl wants to be one, but it's more than just putting on clothes and walking around. The good models—the ones we look for today—have a special relationship with what they're wearing. They change with whatever they put on, and they take on the clothes' identity. What happened the other night—"

"Please, Mr. Taylor, do you have to mention—"

He held up his hand to silence her. "Let me finish. What happened the other night when I saw you... Well, I know women, Vanessa, and I know fashion. I saw what those clothes did to you."

Vanessa hung her head, shame flooding through her again. He'd never understand what a silly, girlish game it had been, how private and embarrassing it was to have been discovered.

Taylor took her wrist and started for the darkened warehouse outside the office and Vanessa had no choice but to follow. "I've just been talking with Cal Everett about the new Dana Falco line for spring. Come on. I want you to try one on."

"Oh Mr. Taylor. No. I couldn't. I don't know anything about modeling."

She continued to protest as he led her out to one of the racks of gowns and threw back the protective plastic cover. The Dana Falco line was high-end evening wear for older women, the kind Taylor had referred to as "society page wear"—expensive fabric, simple cut, elegant and mostly conservative. He selected the youngest-looking dress he could find, a gown of red velvet with long sleeves and a square bodice, almost medieval in cut, simple and unadorned. Vanessa drew back as if it were something dangerous, fascinated and almost frightened. He held it up for her and she approached it again, looking at it carefully in the dim light that spilled onto the dark shop floor from the office.

Her family had never had much money, and Vanessa had always been happy as a tomboy, avoiding the trendier fads her friends had gone through in junior high and high school. The only extravagances she'd ever allowed herself were the whorish, shameful clothes she used for her games of self-stimulation, and even those had been cheap, close-out items sneaked home in her backpack or ordered over the internet and signed for while her mother was at work. The thought that Mr. Taylor wanted her to put on this expensive, handcrafted designer original filled her with a kind of awe and dread.

"Oh my," she said breathlessly. "I don't think I could. Really. I don't think I could."

"Feel the fabric, Vanessa," he said. "Feel it. Italian velvet. They make it special in Turin. It's your size too. Trust me. I know women's bodies. It's made for you."

The material was a velvet of such richness that it almost felt like butter, as smooth as silk on the inside, and warm and yielding on the nap as if it would melt at her touch.

"The changing room's right behind you," he said, offering the gown to her.

As if in a trance Vanessa took the dress and walked into the small room, closed the curtain and turned on the light. She hung the dress up on a hook and stared at it for a moment, thinking of the hands that had stitched it together. She kept her eyes on the dress as she unbuttoned her old flannel shirt and hung it up, then stepped out of her shoes and unbuttoned her jeans and slid them down her legs.

"Take off your bra too," Taylor called from outside.

"What?"

"Don't worry. No one's had this dress on yet. Just do it. The gown's designed to be worn like that."

Vanessa unhooked her bra and slid it off and hung it next to her shirt. She took the dress from the hanger and held it against her, and noticed that she was caressing herself through the fabric, pressing it against her body. Silly. She drew the fabric over her bare arm and then across her chest. The creamy nap of the velvet glided across her bare nipples and the skin of her belly with a delicious intimacy.

Quickly she opened the back zipper and slid the garment down over her head. She got her hands through the sleeves and shimmied it down, her head emerging from the neckline. The fabric had a trace of some exotic smell, perhaps saffron or sandalwood—something exotic and brand new. She tugged it down into place and then ran her hands down over her legs, smoothing it over her thighs. It was just exquisite. She looked up into the mirror and caught her breath. She was beautiful.

She was so entranced by the change in her that she hardly noticed Taylor walking in behind her. Their eyes met in the mirror—hers filled with astonished delight, and his with the level confidence of a man who knew he'd been right. He took the zipper and slid it up the back, pulling the bodice tight around her, then pulled the shoulders straight and adjusted the sleeves.

Vanessa looked at herself in the mirror with something like amazement. She was like a bride, a medieval princess. Taylor reached into her hair and unclipped her barrettes and held them in his teeth, then fluffed her hair free from its ponytail and spread it out over her shoulders. The color of the dress brought out the reddish highlights in her hair and made her skin glow, even under the harsh fluorescents of the changing room. Taylor leaned against the wall with his arms folded and watched her expression, enjoying her pleasure.

"See?" he said. "I know women. I know color. Walk, Vanessa."

"But I don't have any shoes on!" She was still wearing her white cotton socks.

"We'll get you shoes later. Just walk now. Out here." He held the dressing room curtain open for her and Vanessa followed him out onto the dark factory floor.

The velvet caressed her thighs and clung to her stomach and she felt like someone new, as if she were in someone else's skin. She turned and looked back at Taylor and saw that look in his eyes again, the look she'd seen the other night but deeper now—not just lust, but something deeper, more profound. In spite of herself she felt a thrill in her stomach. He found her beautiful.

"Everyone thinks I'm gay," he said softly and smiled. "I'm not. I have a thing about women though, about what they can be and how they look and what that does to the way they feel. Our appearance, Vanessa. It's the key to how we feel about ourselves and who we think we are. Some women are very sensitive to that, aren't they? You're one like that." He looked at her levelly. "We can make you into whatever we want you to be, did you know that, Vanessa? Think of it. Whatever you want to be."

She stood there and heard his words, though she knew she didn't understand. She was too caught up in the way she was feeling in the gown, standing there in the dark warehouse, glowing like a flower in the darkness.

Taylor seemed to read her mind. "How do you feel?" he asked.

Vanessa looked down at herself and noticed the way the skirt subtly revealed her thighs. Her unconfined breasts made proud cones beneath the rich yet clinging fabric.

"I don't know," she said, but they both knew it was a lie. She felt the way she did when she dressed up, only infinitely more sophisticated, more real.

Taylor came over to her and took the lapel of the dress between his fingers. He tested the velvet, running it sensuously between his fingers, and Vanessa felt his touch on the top of her breast.

He was standing right in front of her, inches away, the shadows masking half his face, but the look in his eye was unmistakable.

"Let me tell you how you feel," he said softly. "You feel beautiful. Irresistible. Sexual."

Vanessa heard his words but said nothing, her attention on his hands as they came up and caressed her arms, her shoulders, then slid down her sides to her hips, as if checking the fit of the gown. The fabric was like an extension of her skin, and as he caressed the dress he caressed her as well. They both knew it too.

"There's a test they use for velvet," he whispered, and he smiled. "An old Italian test, traditional, to tell the quality of the fabric. Do you know what it is?"

She shook her head.

"If you can feel a woman's nipples harden beneath the fabric when you stroke them with the back of your fingers, then it's good quality. That's the test."

Vanessa stood there transfixed by his eyes as he let the backs of his fingers glide slowly over the tip of her breast. She gasped softly and felt herself respond, felt the delicious tightening in her breast and the answering response below.

"Mr. Taylor—"

"Shhh," he said. "Keep your arms at your sides, Vanessa."

He repeated the gesture, sliding the backs of his fingers down over her nipple and now she felt the erect bud catch against his fingers as the baby-soft fabric slid over her sensitive flesh.

He raised his other hand but now there was no test. He found her nipple expertly through the fabric and his finger traced a slow circle around her areola, teasing, repeating, 'til Vanessa felt chills race up her spine and the backs of her legs.

She was ready—she was more than ready when he kissed her—her body seeming to fuse to his, her nipples offering themselves shamelessly. Taylor kissed her with all the tenderness and respect due a princess of such beauty and Vanessa stood there with her arms at her sides and let herself be kissed as if it were only right. In a matter of minutes she'd gone from a dumpy college girl in jeans and flannel shirt to a countess in velvet, and his kiss was as different from the hungry savagery of the other night as this exquisite velvet was from the cheap vinyl she'd been wearing then.

He put his hands on the sides of her face and held her tenderly as his lips glided against hers, as if testing her to see if she were real, afraid she might disappear. This was a man's worshipful obeisance to a woman's beauty and Vanessa felt special, special just for him.

This was Mr. Taylor—her boss and a friend her mother's—and now he was kissing her, making a woman out of her, the palpable evidence of his excitement pressing against her stomach. Vanessa was lost, overwhelmed. She opened her mouth and kissed him back, offering him everything. What secrets did she have from him anymore?

Taylor felt the change in her and in one smooth motion reached down and scooped her up into his arms like a child. It was a dramatic, romantic gesture, yet there in the darkened warehouse, dressed in that velvet gown, it felt perfectly appropriate and it made Vanessa's head swim. He carried her across the warehouse floor to his office and she couldn't help but notice her white cotton socks still on her feet, peeking from beneath the velvet. He took her into the office and laid her down on the leather sofa and turned off the lights. The darkness was almost complete, the only light coming from the exit sign above the door.

He stood there at the foot of the sofa 'til Vanessa had to venture a look at him, and she saw the confusion and anguish in his eyes. The other night had been an act of passion, without thought and with Vanessa dressed like she'd already been caught in the act, but this was different—deliberate, intentional, consensual. She saw him fighting with himself as he looked down at her lying there and she didn't know what to do.

"Lift the dress, Vanessa," he said. "Gather it up around your waist."

She did as he said, bunching the gorgeous material up until the hem just covered her privates. Taylor opened his belt, unfastened his button and pulled down his zipper, then pushed his pants and shorts down his legs. He was achingly hard and the sight of his erection made Vanessa's heart leap in her throat. She'd done that to him, and not in her slut clothes this time but in a dress that made her beautiful.

He knelt on the sofa between her open legs, holding his tool in his hand as if to keep it from exploding. He looked at her face and she saw the anguish in his eyes, the struggle he was losing with himself.

"I can't," he said breathlessly. "I just can't. Not now. Not like this. But I have to have you, Vanessa. Do you understand? The way you look. It affects me too, and I can't help myself. I have to, Vanessa, I have to."

She wanted to tell him that it was all right, that she wanted it too, but she had no words, and it was all so much like a dream that she was afraid to speak. Taylor was already pushing her skirt up higher over her hips and her panties, bunching it around her waist. Her bare thighs gleamed in the dim light. Taylor took his shaft in his hand and lowered himself over her, the swollen head striking her panties just between her legs and making her jump. She was so alive down there, so eager and ready, and all he had to do was pull that little strip of fabric to the side or tear her panties off her, she didn't care. But no, he began moving his hips, his jaw clenched, sending the head of his cock sliding against her panty-covered slit.

Vanessa groaned. It was so lewd, so obscene. He wouldn't even fuck her, as if he were already so excited that he couldn't bother to put himself inside her, and instead he pumped the head of his throbbing phallus against her open sex, separated only by the thin fabric of her flowered panties. Vanessa spread her legs, giving him access, understanding now that he wouldn't fuck her but still wanting to give him the pleasure he so desperately needed, a pleasure that ate at her too like delicious acid, denying her the fulfillment she craved but still setting her nerves on edge. She wanted him inside her. She wanted that fullness, but she would have to settle for this trembling, maddening friction.

It almost seemed right. It almost seemed like this was all that a commoner was allowed to do with a princess, as if forbidden to know her hidden treasure of her flesh. Was this her due as well, her punishment for her beauty? Or just the last traces of his guilt for ravishing the girl who'd been like a daughter to him?

"Oh God!" he cried, his voice a strangled cry as he worked his shaft against her crotch, now wet with a combination of their juices.

Vanessa turned her head and could see their reflection in the dark glass of the office window. Taylor lifted her leg over the back of the sofa, opening her even further, and stood with one foot on the floor, the other knee on the sofa. His buttocks flexed and hollowed as he set the bottom of his shaft sliding over her cleft, pressing the fabric into her wet opening. Vanessa moaned. She lifted her hips to him, trying to direct the friction to where she needed it most. He was gasping, his breath racing through his nostrils like a stallion's as he worked his naked cock against the thin fabric of her panties and the sensitive, wanting flesh beneath.

"Oh Christ!" he moaned. "Oh God! Vanessa!"

Just then she found the angle, pressing her bottom down into the leather sofa so that his hard rod scraped against her most sensitive spot. Thrills shot through her body—her legs, her arms—covering her with gooseflesh and she threw her head back in rapture.

It was naughty, obscene. Two wild animals intent on having their fill of each other in this most basic and selfish way. The feel of his hardness against her and his desperate gasps and shuddering thrusts lifted her up and out and into the arms of a devastating orgasm, all the more intense for the pure venality of their actions, and as she gasped out her profane pleasure, she felt Taylor press hard against her. He arched his back, threw his head back and cried out in a growl of terrible anguish, almost pain, then thrust hard and flooded her panties with his hot seed, his hips jerking against her in convulsions of savage, ecstatic release.

His thick ejaculate spattered onto her trembling tummy and Vanessa frantically clawed the dress out of the way of his jets of release. She raised her head to see it emerge from his arching, reaching tool, a sight she'd never seen before. *The urgency! The desperation in the way he ejaculated!* A few hard spurts and then it flooded out in a thick rich stream against the thin panties that covered her aching pussy. She felt herself trembling down there as if reaching desperately for him as he gushed against her in total surrender.

She dug her nails into his arms as he came and was suddenly aware of two things, how terribly strong he was—his arms were like steel bands beneath her fingers—and how he trembled with the force of his release, as if his discharge took all the strength from his body. This was the terrible urgency of real sex, the sheer power, so different from the games she had played in the back seats of cars with boys in high school, so desperate, so consuming.

He was right. She was a woman now, ready or not.

He leaned above her, his forehead pressed against hers as he gasped for breath, and she knew that now it was he who was consumed by guilt, he who had shown her his secret desires and was ashamed. She reached up and caressed the back of his neck, telling him it was all right, that she understood and he had no need to explain.

Mr. Taylor climbed off her, avoiding her eyes. He was panting for breath, as was she, her breasts rising and falling. Taylor took some tissues from the box on the desk and wiped himself off, then tenderly, almost apologetically wiped his come off her belly and her stained panties, wiping her 'til she was clean.

"I'm afraid to move," she said. "I don't want to get it on the dress."

He looked her and smiled kindly. "The hell with the dress," he said. "It's too good for their line anyhow. I think you should have it. They'll never miss it."

She looked at his face in the dark, for so long he'd been someone to idealize—someone remote and powerful and belonging to that mysterious world of adult success Vanessa had so wanted to join. She'd had a secret crush on him, a crush that had lasted so long she'd come to take it for granted. She remembered how hurt she'd been when she came to work for him and saw the kinds of women who came by his shop—her competition, way out of her league. It had been foolish of course, but still she'd been hurt.

Now she tried to see him anew, as a man and a lover, his handsome face slack with sexual satisfaction and tinged with shame. He could have taken her again if he'd wanted. He could have tied her up and fucked her and done whatever he wanted to her and she would have let him. Even as it was, she knew she had pleased him. He wasn't so old anymore, nor was she so young. The idea thrilled her.

"Are we lovers now, Mr. Taylor?"

"Rob," he corrected. "You can call me Rob now, I think." He crumpled the tissue then turned and brushed her hair out of her eyes. He looked at her in the darkness and she saw things in his eyes she knew she wasn't old enough to understand. What he'd done to her had been so thrilling and she felt no guilt at all, not like last time. Why did he seem so sad?

"Is that what you want, Vanessa?"

She didn't know. She suddenly didn't seem to know anything, except that what he did to her was thrilling and now she felt no remorse.

She changed back into her clothes and left the velvet gown hanging in the changing room and Rob locked up the warehouse and walked her downstairs, all in silence. He offered to drive her home, but it wasn't that late and she lived only a few blocks away and she wanted to walk.

There was a moment of awkwardness when she wondered whether she should kiss him good night, but by then they were on the street and he didn't offer, just busied himself locking up the burglar gates and arming the alarm on the shop.

Vanessa hefted her book bag up on her shoulder. Out of the gown now, she felt like her old self and already what had happened upstairs seemed like a dream, like a movie she'd seen or something she'd imagined. She waited for him to say something, to give her some explanation, but he just walked to his car and opened the door, then stood there, one foot inside, looking at her.

She raised her face inquiringly and he smiled again, that same sad smile.

"We're the same, you and I," he said. "You don't know how true that is, Vanessa. But I do. It's amazing how alike we are."

Chapter Three

೮೨

This time there was no fooling herself about what had happened and what she'd felt, or about there being some sort of relationship with Mr. Taylor. She knew it was awkward, but just how and why it she couldn't quite say. Was it because of their ages? The clothes? Was it a game? Vanessa had no one to talk to about these things, and even if she had, she knew that this whole confusing mess was somehow tied up with her first game of dress-up, a subject she was not willing to discuss with anyone.

Her schoolwork helped. She'd always been able to shut out the world when she was able to concentrate on the mathematics she loved—neat, logical, beautiful and so pleasing the way everything fit together. And it was while doing some math homework that she realized, whatever it was between them, she had to stop it. If it meant quitting her job with him, if it meant losing his financial help, she would just have to put up with it, because the things he did to her and the things he made her feel were just too much for her to handle right now and she knew they must be wrong. She would end it and her main problem became how she would tell him—that wouldn't be hard. A letter of resignation would probably do. He'd always been a gentleman at heart. And, worse—what she would tell her mother, would she understand? She was sure she would think of something and in the meantime she had her schoolwork. She wasn't due back at work 'til Wednesday to pick up the accounts, so she had time to think.

So when the doorbell rang on Monday night, interrupting their dinner, and she heard his voice at the door, she was seized by a sudden panic. She and her sister Cheryl were arguing over some nonsense and her mother got up to answer it. She heard her mother in friendly conversation with someone—a neighbor probably—and she paid no attention until she heard his voice and realized it was him.

"No, no, Rob, we're just finishing dinner," her mother said from the hallway. "Come on in, come in, you can ask her yourself."

Vanessa's face must have gone white, judging by the way Cheryl looked at her, and when she turned around, there he was, standing in the very kitchen where he'd discovered her in her vinyl whore's dress almost a week ago. He was wearing the same jacket and he had the same easy smile but she caught the look of intimate knowledge he gave her. She thought her heart would stop. She couldn't look at him and turned back to her plate.

"Girls, look who's here," her mother said. Turning to Mr. Taylor, she said, "Rob, you must have something to eat." Since his divorce, Mrs. Wallace worried that he had no one to cook for him.

"Hi, Cheryl," he said, shaking her hand with a smile. "Vanessa," he said, and she held out her hand and felt him squeeze it, his fingers lingering just a bit too long as he let her hand go. "No, no, really. I just ate, in fact, and I can't stay."

Vanessa's face was red now and her blood pounded in her ears. From the look in Cheryl's eyes Vanessa could tell that she thought Mr. Taylor was hunky, even if he was closer to her mother's age than her own. But then Cheryl had always been a flirt.

"Mr. Taylor's got another job for you, Vanessa. I told him you'd be glad to help."

He smiled again and said, "Well, it's really not all that big a deal. I'm just going away overnight tomorrow and I need someone to keep an eye on the dog. Leroy will tear the place up if there's no one there to keep him company and I really don't want to board him for a night, it all came up so sudden.

So if Vanessa could just spend the night over there that would be great. I'd pay you, of course."

"Uh, tomorrow I can't," she said nervously. "I made other plans."

Her mom looked at her with exasperation. "What plans? You didn't tell me about any plans."

"With some of the kids at school. We're going to…er…get together and study." Vanessa was a terrible liar, especially in front of her mother.

"Well, you're always complaining about not having any money," her mother said now. "You could cancel your plans. Or study over at Mr. Taylor's house. I'm sure he wouldn't mind, would you, Rob?"

"Not at all," he said. "The more the merrier and I'm sure Vanessa's college friends are as well-behaved as she is."

He knew perfectly well she wouldn't invite any friends.

"I'll do it!" Cheryl volunteered. Her eagerness made the grownups laugh.

"You're still grounded for that F in French," her mother said. "Besides Mr. Taylor asked for Vanessa. She's the responsible one."

Vanessa had been avoiding his eyes, but she couldn't keep this up without looking suspicious. She searched desperately for an excuse to get out of it, but she couldn't think of anything. Her mother was looking at her. She had to say something.

"Okay."

"Good," her mom said. "What time do you want her?"

"About seven or eight would be fine."

It seemed settled. Mr. Taylor and her mother talked on about his fictitious plans—some overnight beauty expo or something—all nonsense, all lies and fabrication. Vanessa sat there feeling chills and at the same time, some strange hunger grew in her stomach and between her legs. She knew what would happen at his house.

Mr. Taylor smiled and said goodbye and Mrs. Wallace walked him out to the hallway then called to her.

"Vanessa? Vanessa, Mr. Taylor wants to know what kind of food you'd like to eat."

Vanessa had gotten up to take her plate to the sink, her appetite gone. "What?"

Her mother came back in and pulled her out into the hallway as if she were bundling her off on a date and whispered urgently to her. "Go talk to him. Stop being so rude to the poor man. He wants to pay you just for helping him out. After all he does for you too!"

Reluctantly Vanessa walked up to him where he stood by the front door.

"I just wanted to know what you like to eat, for snacks and things," he said innocently. Vanessa kept her eyes down.

She shrugged. Something made her look at him though. As if against her will, she raised her eyes and looked into his and her façade of cold anger couldn't stand up under his gaze.

He had some hold over her. She tried to show him resentment and anger when she looked at him, but he saw past that and right into her. It was that look again. That look of naked desire and a look of knowledge. *He knew who she was! He knew her better than she knew herself!* And tomorrow night he was going to teach her some more.

All the resistance melted from her, leaving a hollow thrill in her stomach. "Tomorrow night," he said softly. Then he called into the kitchen in a cheery voice. "Good night, Cheryl, Jenna. Sorry I can't stay."

He looked at Vanessa once more and smiled, then left.

She wouldn't go, she thought. She'd make herself sick, or she'd go spend the night at a friend's house and lie if she had to. But she knew she couldn't. She was such a bad liar.

In fact, she was such a bad liar that when her mother offered to drop her off at Mr. Taylor's on the way to her night class Vanessa could find no way out of it. Her mind raced even as she threw some overnight things into a backpack as her mother waited impatiently.

"Your toothbrush? Don't you want your toothbrush? And your books? You're not going to take your books? Are your friends coming over?"

"No, no," Vanessa said irritably as she threw some texts into her book bag. As if she would ever look at them.

Good mother that she was, her mom even waited to make sure that Vanessa got into Mr. Taylor's house safely before driving away.

He was wearing a shirt and tie when he let her in, and despite her numbness she realized that he looked very good. Leroy the dog slept in the corner by the heater as he always did. If there was ever a dog that needed less watching than Leroy, Vanessa had never met it. The dog would sleep through an earthquake. He didn't even raise his head to look at her when she came in.

She might have enjoyed this. If he hadn't manipulated the situation, if he hadn't forced her to lie. But then how else would he have arranged this without lying to her mother? She'd made up her mind that it was over, but now, with the opportunity to have time alone with him, what choice did she have? She couldn't just walk away.

He locked the door after her and pocketed the key—she was trapped.

"Don't," was all she could say as she stood in his living room, "Mr. Taylor, I don't know what you think, but what we've been doing isn't right. We can't do this anymore."

"I'm disappointed," he said, looking her up and down. "Jeans and a sweater? I thought you'd do better than that."

She stood in the middle of the living room still wearing her leather jacket as he walked around her, appraising her.

"Mr. Taylor, really. This isn't right. You came in that night and found me fooling around, trying on some clothes I had. Just fooling around. And then in the warehouse… Well, I don't know what happened. But I'm not like that really. I'm not that kind of girl. I don't do this—certainly not with someone old enough to be my own father." She was sorry she'd said it as soon as the words were out of her mouth, but he didn't seem to mind.

"It's not right," she said again. "You caught me at a weak moment…"

He sat down on the arm of the sofa and idly played with a piece of rope. She realized now that there were all sorts of things on the sofa—rope, leather cuffs, gags, vibrators—a whole collection. Her stomach did a little flip and she felt a thrill run up her spine. He had a collection much like hers, though larger, more expensive and sophisticated, and there seemed to be everything there—leather and chrome and plastic and chain, the most wicked and heinous-looking sexual devices.

"I figured you wouldn't be able to bring your toys," he said, "so these are mine. We have similar tastes."

"Mr. Taylor—"

"Hey, I just thought we might play together," he said, looking at her pointedly. "You know, just fool around. I even bought you some clothes. Want to see?"

"I've got to go," she said. She turned and strode to the front door. "Open the door please."

He watched her from the sofa, playing with the rope. That light was back in his eyes and she was afraid to look at him.

"You can stop that, Vanessa," he said softly. "You can just stop all that crap. You know you loved it. You loved it in your bedroom and you loved it in the warehouse. You loved every bit of it, didn't you?"

49

She stood at the door, her hand on the knob, her forehead pressed against the wood as if in defeat. "Please unlock the door, Mr. Taylor."

He got up off the sofa and walked toward her slowly. "I told you that you were just like me, remember, Vanessa? The look. The way you dress is the way you feel. I understand that. I thought we might explore a little further."

She was trying not to listen, because what he was saying was filling her with shame and excitement at the same time. "No," she said, "No. You're wrong. I'm not like that. It was a game."

"Yes it was a game," he said. "And it was more than that too, wasn't it? Behind every game there's a little truth. That's why we play them. To pretend, to slip into that other role for just a taste, just to see what it's like."

He came up to her now and took her arm, turned her around and pinned her against the door with his body, his face inches from hers. She shook her head, her eyes closed tight.

Just as he had that first fateful day, he took her wrists in his hands and lifted them over her head, pressing them against the door. He leaned his weight against her and she gasped as she felt the hard stalk of his cock dig into her stomach.

"That wasn't just some little game you were playing that first night. You were trying out the role, weren't you? You liked dressing up like that. Just a hot little tease. I saw the stuff in your bedroom—the rope, the handcuffs and whips," he said as he wrapped the rope around her wrist. "So why don't you just admit it so we can get on with our show?"

He had her wrists bound together now and he pulled her back into the living room, the feel of the rope on her wrists was so thrilling that she almost sobbed in shame and excitement. It set her free somehow—it absolved her of responsibility. Tears welled up in her eyes and she tried to fight him, tried to free her wrists, but he pulled her around and threw her roughly down on the sofa.

Before she could move he was on top of her, one hand holding her wrists out of the way, the other pushing her jacket aside and pulling up her sweater. She tried to break free but his hand closed on her breast and squeezed hard, making her cry out. He grabbed her bra and pulled it down so that her breasts fell free, then he sucked one into his mouth as she arched off the couch, trying to throw him off.

"Stop it! Stop it!" she cried out, but he held her down and his free hand scrabbled at her jeans, trying to get them open. She tossed her hips, trying to get away from him, but she felt his strong fingers open her pants, then the zipper, then his hand was sliding inside her panties.

When his finger touched her flesh they both froze, as if they knew they were poised at the critical point, that after this there was no going back, no retreat. Then he slowly pushed his finger against her and she let out a moan of shame. She was aroused and wet and she knew it, and now he knew it too—he could feel it. Everything he'd said had been true. She couldn't deny it now, her body wouldn't let her. His finger slid easily along her soaking crease then he pulled his hand out and showed her his glistening finger.

"Look at that," he said in mock surprise as she turned her head away in humiliation. "Look at that, Vanessa. You're already wet. You're on fire, aren't you? Now taste it!"

"Mr. Taylor, no—"

He pushed his finger against her mouth. "Suck it, Vanessa. I want you to taste your own excitement. Suck it!"

She opened her mouth, embarrassment racking her body, and she let him put his sticky finger in her mouth. She tasted her own musk, the undeniable proof of all he had said about her, the taste of her shame.

"So you're a hot little tease, Vanessa," he said as he slid his finger back into her panties and began to rub her slit again. "That's not so bad. I know you can't help it, can you, baby?

Your body just won't behave. See? You're already pushing that little pussy against my hand, aren't you?"

She gasped. He was right—she'd been humping her hips against his hand as if fucking it. She hadn't realized that she'd been doing it. It was like her body had a mind of its own. She made herself stop.

"It just feels so good, doesn't it, Vanessa? It feels so good to have someone touch you and kiss you, someone to want you so much," he said as he continued to kiss her breasts and finger her. "You can't help it. It's natural, a part of who you are. Don't ignore it, Vanessa. Don't deny it. You need someone who knows what you want, that's all, and I'm that person."

She still had her head turned to the side, trying to hide her face from him. She didn't believe him. It wasn't true. She was a straight-A student. Not that she was a prude, it was just that she was so busy studying. She dated when she had time, and she'd made love before. It's not like she wasn't aware of her sexuality, but everything was so confusing now—the way his words excited her—it was far more than she had ever felt before.

But his fingers and his mouth felt so good, and she loved the way he pressed her down, her arms tied and held out of the way. There was no way she could fight him as he kissed her breasts and stomach and played with her excited pussy. None of the guys she'd dated had ever treated her this way. They didn't have a beard that scraped on her tender skin, and none of them had a mouth that was so hot and demanding for her, a mouth that had already known so many women's bodies and now wanted hers. Her lovers never forced her down and told her what she was right to her face, shaming her and making her wild with excitement. Her dates were just boys— Mr. Taylor was a man. It made all the difference in the world.

He was pushing her back into the cushions of the sofa and her little moans of protest were taking on a different meaning as he sucked a nipple into his mouth and lashed it with his tongue. His finger was teasing at her sex, rimming her hole, and she wanted him to stick it inside her. He was driving her crazy.

He caught her nipple between his teeth and bit down on it, not too hard, but hard enough to send a spear of pleasure-pain shooting through her body and igniting a sudden gush of masochistic pleasure.

"Oh God!" she cried out as she thrust her hips up against his hand. Her own body was betraying her, humiliating her. Her body wanted more. Her body loved being treated like this, taking over where her mind wouldn't always let her go.

Suddenly he got off her and stood up, leaving her lying there panting with her sweater pulled up over her chest and her pants gaping open. He pulled her up into a sitting position and untied her wrists.

Vanessa was confused, groggy, her head reeling from her sensual excitement as she tried to understand what was happening to her. Was he done? Why had he stopped? He pulled her to her feet and, with her wrists free, she ran a hand through her tousled hair, trying to calm down and get her bearings.

"Take your coat off," he said, and she realized that she was still wearing her leather jacket. She slipped it off and just dropped it on the floor, something she would never do at home. But she was dizzy and not herself and there was something in his voice that made her eager to obey. She was a stranger to all this, but he knew what he was doing.

"Now take your clothes off," he said as he sat back down on the sofa.

She looked at him in surprise. Her clothes? Her pants were hanging open, her panties showing, and her breasts were still naked, her bra was twisted and pushed down out of the way. Her nipple still ached where he had bitten it and she could feel his saliva cooling on her skin, but she couldn't undress in front of him. She felt a pang of awkwardness—she was not practiced in stripping for a man—worrying she would loose the aura of power she got from the rush of her sexuality.

The blinds were closed tight. She looked around the room as if seeing it for the first time—the television, the sofa, tables, Leroy snoozing in the corner, all the usual accoutrements of middle-class life. This was where Mr. Taylor had lived with his wife before the divorce, and her womanly touches were everywhere—the pictures on the wall, the knickknacks on the shelves. Vanessa couldn't believe this was happening.

"I can't."

"Yes you can," he said mildly. "And you will, right now. You will because I want to show you something about yourself."

She looked at him in confusion, not understanding, and that was a mistake. She was caught in the force of his gaze, that power he seemed to have over her that told her he knew things about herself that she didn't.

Keeping her head down and burning with shame, she pushed her jeans down over her hips, down her legs and stepped out of them. She lifted her sweater over her head and let it fall as well. He bra wasn't doing her any good so she started to unfasten that too when he said, "Okay. Stop there. Now look at yourself."

She was already looking down, but she didn't understand what she was supposed to see.

He said, "You knew you were coming over here tonight, didn't you, Vanessa? Of course you did. And look at the underwear you wore."

She looked down. She was wearing one of her favorite pair of pale blue panties, very tiny and very sexy, and her matching bra, just a whisper of thin fabric that she'd spent more on than she ever should have. It was her sexiest ensemble outside of her special clothes. She remembered getting dressed to come over here. She'd painstakingly showered and dressed. Why had she chosen to wear these from her underwear drawer? If she was honest with herself, she had wanted to feel sexy. She had wanted to look sexy for him.

"You wear stuff like that every day?" he asked her with a laugh.

Her face went red and her embarrassment made her suddenly conscious that she was standing there mostly naked. She grabbed her bra and twisted it around to cover her breasts. Mr. Taylor got up and quickly picked up her jeans and sweater and tucked them under his arm.

"Your clothes are in there," he said, pointing to the den. "I laid them all out for you. Bought them special."

She had a fear of seeing those clothes. Whatever they were, she knew what they would do to her when she put them on. She had to get out of there. She thought about grabbing her coat and trying to make a dash for it, but the door was locked. She stood there, frozen with indecision.

That was all it took for him to lose his temper. He threw her clothes in a wad against the wall, strode over to her and took her arm.

"Listen, Vanessa, let's not screw around! You're not fooling anyone with that innocent act, not even yourself, so why don't you drop it? Face it, darling—I know who you are and I know what you want and it's waiting for you right through those doors."

She tried to struggle away from him but he twisted her arms behind her back. He gathered both her wrists into one massive hand and kept her arms pinned behind her as he pulled her to him and reached down to shove his hand between her legs again.

She groaned in anger and frustration as she felt him touch her but he held her hands immobile. He was too strong and he handled her effortlessly, as if she were a child. His free hand ran along her body, cupping her breasts and finally pulling her face around to his and he kissed her hard.

It was no use. The struggling just seemed to make them both hotter. The feel of his strength and his obvious desire for her made her weak and the more she tried to hide it, the more urgently she wanted to feel him against her, holding her, not letting her go. She wanted him to force her to do everything for him. She wanted him to push her down and take her, make her do things, make her do every filthy thing she'd ever dreamed of.

He broke the kiss but held her face in his hand. "You're going to go in there and you're going to put on those clothes and then we'll see if I'm right about you, Vanessa, if you're who I think you are. It's just like your dress-up game, but this time I'm playing too. Then you're going to come out here and show me your hot little ass, and you're going to do whatever I tell you to do. If I tell you to suck my cock, you'll get down on your knees and suck my cock. If I tell you to play with yourself, you're going to play with yourself. If I tell you to spread your legs and show me your little pussy, you're going to spread your legs and show me your pussy. And you know what else? You're going to love it! You're going to just fucking love it! So quit acting like you're too good for this and let's get moving."

His words cut into her like daggers, each one dripping with his hot need. At the end of his speech he pulled her to him and kissed her again, slipping his hand beneath her panties to cup her ass. One finger dipped low and poked against her tiny asshole and the lewdness of his touch made her squeal into his mouth as her sex throbbed with hungry desire.

He propelled her to the den and pushed her inside, her head reeling. The clothes were laid out on the sofa and even as she looked at them with horror her pulse began to race. There were a pair of sandals with enormous heels, a tiny miniskirt of some stretchy gold metallic fabric and a skimpy red tank top about the size of a washcloth, very sheer and elastic. They were lewd, whorish—far worse than anything she would have picked for herself, but just the sight of them made her pulse race. He knew her like a book and the knowledge thrilled her.

"And take off your underwear," he called from the other room. "No bra, no panties."

Half in a daze, she stripped off her clothes and began to dress in what he'd left for her. The miniskirt was tight. As she zipped it up she felt it compress her buttocks together, and she could see her pubic mound where it puffed out the front just a bit. The top was tiny and so tight and sheer that even the areolas on her breasts were visible. The top looked as though it was sprayed on.

But it wasn't until she put the shoes on that she really felt the part. They raised her up, pushed her ass out and made her throw her shoulders back for balance. There was no mirror down here, but she could imagine what she looked like and it thrilled her. She looked cheap and on display, pure sex waiting to be used, just like she'd always fantasized.

She was afraid to face him. What if he laughed? As naughty as she felt, a part of her was still Vanessa, the good little straight-A student trying to play the bad girl. What if he laughed?

"I'm waiting," he called.

She took a deep breath to try to calm herself, then she walked into the living room.

When she saw the look in his eyes her fears melted, replaced by an incandescent glow of excitement. There was a gleam in his eye, sharp and bright, almost violent, and a nasty smile on his face that gave her goose bumps. It was that look of want and naked desire, but purer now that they were in his house with the door locked and no distractions, no fear of being interrupted. He glared at her so intently that her excitement was tinged with a bit of fear, as if he might suddenly attack her. He looked as if he were ready to.

This was the way men looked at her in her fantasies before they threw her on the bed and ravished her, but in her fantasies she was always somewhat in control, always the femme fatale. This was real and she felt more naked than if she'd had no clothes on at all. Still, the feeling was thrilling and delicious. It made her feel intoxicated and powerful in a way that surprised her.

"Walk," he said simply, his voice hardly more than a dry whisper.

She felt like the goddess of lust. She walked and felt her hips slide inside the slippery metallic skirt. Her nipples were hard and rubbed teasingly against the tight fabric of the top. From the height of her heels she no longer felt like a student drudge but tall and adult—sexy and dangerous, and her feelings were only reinforced by what she saw in his eyes. This was the difference between playing alone and sharing a fantasy with someone else, someone who felt exactly as she did and shared her every emotion.

She was filled with a confidence and sense of power like she'd never felt before and she didn't even wobble as she walked across the floor in the unfamiliar shoes. She stopped and, without giving it a thought, spun like a runway model and pulled it off flawlessly, then stopped and let him have a good look at her in profile.

She was so keyed up she was afraid she might giggle with sheer pleasure and the look of raw lust on his face was so extreme it was almost amusing. She had a sudden urge to tease him. Her fear and resistance were gone now, as if the power had shifted from him to her and she was calling the shots now. It was a heady and delirious feeling.

She made a show of doing something with her hair so that she could raise her arms, hiking up her breasts so they hung rich and full on her chest and he just sat there and stared. She could see his cock tenting the front of his pants, could almost see it pulsing with his heartbeat and on impulse she turned her back to him and bent over, putting her hands on her knees and causing her skirt to rise up in the back and showing just a hint of the bottom of her ass and her puff of pubic hair where it showed through her legs.

She heard him literally gasp—a sharp intake of breath through his nose—and she smiled to herself.

"Don't you think this skirt is too short?" she asked innocently.

"Come here," he breathed, and Vanessa couldn't repress a giggle. "Come over here."

This is how she'd always wanted to feel—irresistibly sexy and powerful enough to keep a man under her thumb just by his wanting her. She liked walking on the edge, never knowing when she might push him so far that he'd explode, grab her and force her to do all sorts of terrible, obscene things.

As she walked over to him, she suddenly felt conscious of their difference in age. She was young, not even out of school, at the very peak of her body's ripeness. He was old enough to be her father, experienced and supposedly mature enough to control his feelings. She felt like a little slave girl who'd caught the fancy of the old and powerful king and she liked the feeling. His age added a taste of the forbidden. This was no horny boy she was playing with. This man was dangerous.

He reached out and grabbed her wrist, pulled her into his lap and she fell on him with a little squeal of alarm. He pressed his face against her breasts and his hand slid right up under her skirt to her naked sex, puffy with excitement and ready to be used.

"You little tramp!" he hissed at her. "What happened to the good girl now, huh? What happened to the good little Vanessa?"

She laughed with excitement as his hand stroked between her legs and he licked at her nipple through the top.

"I lied," she said delightedly. "I am a tease. But what are you going to do about it, Mr. Taylor? Teach me a lesson?"

The words came easily to her, even as she shocked herself by saying them. It was just like her dress-up game only real.

Those were the kinds of things she said to her imaginary lovers when she would look in the mirror and pose for herself, imagining their eyes hot with desire.

He grabbed her face in his hand and kissed her roughly, his beard scratching her as he spread her legs and pushed a thick finger into her. She gasped as it slid in easily.

"Mmmmm!" She moaned into his mouth, pushing her hips forward against his hand as she felt him enter her. His touch felt so good—his roughness was like an aphrodisiac and she opened her thighs before squeezing them tightly around his hand. She wanted it like this. She was a tease and she needed to be punished for acting this way. She needed his violence. It thrilled her.

"Stand up!" he said and he pushed her off his lap as she mewled with disappointment. He stood up and spun her around so her back was to him and she felt him wrapping rope around her wrists yet again.

She was disappointed, wanting to tease him even more, but at the same time she loved the rope. She loved being bound and helpless, unable to defend herself, and she loved the way being bound pushed her chest out. She knew it just increased his lust too, just made him hotter and wilder, and when he spun her back around to face him she had the nerve to give him a sultry little pout.

That was going too far, and he grabbed her hair and pulled her head back roughly.

"You want to play games?" he hissed at her as his free hand roamed over her body, squeezing her breasts and pinching her nipples, sliding over her stomach to stroke her pussy. "Well, you don't play games with me, Vanessa. I know women. I design them and make them what they are. And I know you and what you are, hiding behind that innocent little college girl while you're burning for it inside. You're just dying to be treated like a little tramp, aren't you? You're just dying to be used by a man who knows what he wants. You want to be made to pay, don't you?"

His words made her gasp. She loved it. She closed her eyes and bit her lip and let them wash over her like the hot spray of a shower, basking in their obscene heat.

"Well, you know what's going to happen to you, baby?" he went on, whispering in her ear so close she could feel his hot breath, "I'm going to tie you up good and tight and see just what kind of girl you are. I'm going to shove my big, hard cock in you, Vanessa, and I'm going to fuck the hell out of you! Fuck you hard, baby—hard and deep, stretch that little pussy wide open and give you exactly what you've been asking for."

She groaned at the force of his words and he pulled her head back again.

"And then you're going to suck my cock, open that sweet mouth and take me in your mouth and suck on me. Every good tramp loves to suck cock, doesn't she, baby, and I already know you're real good. You'll suck my cock 'til I shoot my come all over your gorgeous face and then you'll wipe it all up and swallow it.

"But first," he said, "I've got something else for you."

She was on fire now and she needed him badly. Her hips had started moving of their own accord, trying to rub against him, and she felt all liquid and buttery inside. He let go of her hair, turned and dropped his pants, groaning with relief as his cock was able to spring free inside his shorts. He kicked off his shoes and socks and slid his trousers off his legs, revealing a pair of powerful thighs. Vanessa saw the wet spot on the front of his shorts and her nostrils flared as she imagined his tool in her mouth, how depraved it would look.

He sat down with his shorts still on and pulled her down. She went to sit on his lap again but he spun her around somehow, manhandling her until she was over his knee and she realized that he was going to spank her.

This was something she'd never envisioned in her games and this time she felt real alarm as he slid her miniskirt up over her naked bottom.

"Wait! Mr. Taylor! Wait!" but he held her down with his arm in the small of her back and with her hands tied behind her there was nothing she could do.

In her whole life she'd never been hit and it was degrading to be treated like a child and taken over his knee when she'd just been feeling like such an adult. Degrading, but there was something in her very helplessness that stoked the fire within in her and made her wait breathlessly for the first display of his angry male lust.

"You know why you're getting this?" he asked her as he squeezed her naked cheeks. "Because you're such a fucking tease, Vanessa! You're totally out of control. You get all dressed up like that and you'll do anything for cock, won't you?"

Before she could even decide to answer she felt rather than saw him raise his hand and he brought it down with a loud smack on her ass, making her squeal and sending a surge of heat through her body. He spanked her again and she jumped, her eyes wide.

She could feel his erection pressing into her stomach, rock-hard as she tried to protect her behind with her tied hands, but he just spanked her again and again until all she felt was a generalized burning that melted into the hot need that throbbed between her legs. But worse than the pain was the very humiliation of being treated this way, humiliation that built her excitement even higher. She loved his male power and strength, the way he took no grief from her, the way he made her hurt.

After a few spanks she stopped struggling, waiting for every blow, each slap like a thrust of pleasure into her sex. Her squeals of alarm became a low, throaty moan of gratification as her hips began to grind against the hardness in his lap, showing him what she needed, showing him she was ready.

And it was only fair after the way she'd teased and taunted him. She deserved it, and she was glad he was there to give it to her. She loved it. She loved teasing him and seeing the wild lust in his eyes and there was nothing she could do but take her punishment for her own filthy desires. Each slap on her naked and trembling ass only made her hotter, made her think of even filthier things she wanted him to make her do.

Then suddenly she was on her knees on the floor and he was standing over her. He skinned his shorts down and she saw his gorgeous cock, big and stiff and so swollen it looked like the skin might split, his big balls hanging below. She hadn't really looked at it before, either in her bedroom or in the warehouse, but now she looked and studied it and felt her throat constrict with desire. This wasn't the bright eager stalk of a boy, but a man's veteran piece, thick and experienced and rough-looking, covered with veins and ridges like a club, almost scary.

He pushed it against her lips and she opened her mouth and tilted her head back as he slid it over her tongue and she felt the bulk fill her up. He tasted salty and musky and she closed her eyes and explored him as far as she could with her tongue.

"Come on, Vanessa!" he said. "You know how to do it! Suck me!"

He had done this before, when he took her on her own bed, and she remembered the deliciously thick, hard, male feel of him in her mouth. But she was on her knees now, kneeling like a slave before him, and that made this even more exciting.

She'd only begun though when he pulled his cock from her mouth, leaving her panting and bewildered. He grabbed her arm and started to pull her to her feet.

"Come on," he said. "We're going to the bedroom."

"Why?" she said. "Fuck me here. Fuck me on the floor."

He laughed and lifted her to her feet. "You giving the orders now? On your feet."

In her heels she was as tall as him, maybe taller. The red tank top was already sweated through between her breasts and on her back, and her bottom was bright red from the spanking. She let him propel her by the arm out of the living room and across the hallway, her heels rapping sharply on the hardwood floor. She climbed the stairs to the second floor unsteadily, his hand on her arm.

Vanessa was dizzy with arousal, her head swimming and her pussy achy and throbbing. Her ass hurt from the spanking and she staggered slightly as he led her down the hallway upstairs, her hands tied behind her. They passed what had been his kids' rooms, his kids who now lived with their mother. She got a glance of the emptiness, the furniture gone, the emptiness of his life. He steered her down to his own bedroom—the one he'd shared with his wife.

There were family pictures on the walls, on the dressers, and as she stood there she felt a bit out of place. This was the bed where he'd slept with his wife—their marriage bed—and Vanessa felt a salacious thrill when she realized that she was taking his wife's place, about to give him what he obviously couldn't get from the other woman. It made her feel hot and wicked and ready to do anything he desired.

He came up to her and grabbed her by the shoulders, pulled her savagely to him and kissed her hard, shoving his tongue into her mouth, and she sucked on it like she had sucked on him before.

"Fuck me!" she said as he pulled away. "Fuck me!"

He spun her around so that she was facing the mirror over the dresser and she looked at herself in shock, her hair a mess, her arms pinned behind her back, the tiny skirt barely covering her sex. Her lips were swollen with desire and her eyes hazy with lust. She was a tramp, a mistress, a sex-doll, and she was proud to see herself that way.

She watched in the mirror as his hands came around her and closed over her straining breasts. He took her nipples between his fingers and squeezed, slowly at first then harder, until pain shot through her body and she hunched her shoulders forward defensively.

64

"You like that, don't you?" he said as he let her go. "You like it when I hurt you."

"No," she said, her voice a husky whisper. "No. Just fuck me! I want it."

He pushed her onto the bed and she fell on her back. Immediately he was between her legs, sliding the miniskirt up over her hips. He held himself up on his extended arms and she looked up into his hard, determined face.

She knew what he was seeing, and she couldn't resist teasing him one last time, inviting his savagery. She stuck her tongue out and waggled it at him invitingly, a gesture from her game, intended to make herself look even sluttier than she already did. It had its effect and she saw desire burn like rage in his eyes.

"I'm going to fuck you now," he said. "I'm going to fuck your pussy and then I'm going to fuck your ass."

"Yes!" she cooed. She looked straight into his eyes and without a hint of shame she said, "Fuck my pussy and fuck my ass. Do it all to me, Mr. Taylor. Fuck me everywhere. I want it all."

He took a deep breath through his nose, thrust his hips forward and impaled her on his cock, shoving his rod right through the fleshy sleeve of her pussy, all the way in.

Vanessa cried out and arched up to him as though she'd been jolted with electricity. Her hips lunged up off the bed so that only her head and heels still touched the mattress, driving herself up over his plunging cock, wanting it, wanting all of it.

"Oh God!" she gasped as he pushed into her — so hard, so demanding. He felt huge and thick — massive, and she felt tiny beneath him, open and defenseless.

She fell back to the mattress and Taylor grabbed her ass and pulled her up to him, shoving into her and snapping his hips hard at the down stroke to make her drive the air from her lungs with a bestial grunt of pleasure. She was tight around him, her vagina swollen and turgid with blood, her muscles quivering as they tried to adjust to his size.

She couldn't hide the pleasure she felt, not only physical, as she pictured what she must look like with her arms tied behind her back, her skirt gathered around her waist and her young thighs wide open, Mr. Taylor's big cock stuffed inside her tiny pussy.

He was brutal with her and she loved it, knowing instinctively it was a sign of his desire, his lust for her, and when he kissed her she bit his lips feverishly and moaned out her submissive pleasure into his open mouth, gasping as his fingers dug into her flesh.

With her arms tied and trapped beneath her there was nothing she could do but let herself be fucked by this violent man and she spread her legs wide and pressed her loins up against him, arching her breasts up against his chest. His weight pressed her down into the mattress so hard she could scarcely breathe and she had to break the kiss to gasp desperately for breath.

Turning her head, she could just see their reflection in the mirror, see his naked, muscular ass flex obscenely as he drove his shaft into her and see her own feet still in those streetwalker's shoes shake with each savage thrust. It was masochistic heaven—she'd never felt so used, so filled, so totally fucked, as if she had a wild bull between her legs, as if she were astride a wild stallion.

Her excitement quickly climbed to the breaking point, egged on by the sight of herself in the mirror, and when he grabbed her nipples again and twisted them she thrilled as the pain seared her body, exploding into a wet little orgasm that she choked back by biting her lip.

A few minutes of this savage pounding and he pulled out of her, leaving her empty and pouting hungrily after him, twitching with the loss of his big rod. She opened her eyes to see him reaching for a jar on the nightstand, scooping up some gel onto his fingers, some lubricant. But her attention was on his big, heavy cock, glistening with her own juices as it throbbed before her, and she thrilled when fell atop her and shoved it back in, blotting out any thoughts as he stretched and filled her once again.

As he fucked her he ran his hand below her ass and she felt his fingers reaching up beneath her toward her pussy. There was the kiss of something cold against her anus and then his finger was pressing against her there, pushing her most intimate spot before it slid inside, making her cry out again.

"Oh yes!" she wailed. "Put your finger in my ass! Do it to me!"

It was wonderfully degrading, the thought of him assaulting her ass, this feeling of fullness in her bowels as his cock slithered in and out of her pussy. His finger was in her bottom, violating her, showing her no respect, worming around and stretching her out, and she'd never felt anything so nasty, so lewd and wonderfully dirty.

"You like that?" he panted in her ear. "You like my fingers in your ass? You do, don't you? Don't you?"

"Yes!" she moaned. "It's good! I love it! Fuck me!"

"You're my little tramp now, aren't you, baby? You're my own little tramp!"

His finger slid farther into her and sparks went off in her brain. "Oh yes! I'm yours, I'm yours! Do whatever you want to me! Do everything!"

She extended her tongue obscenely and let him take it between his lips and suck on it as he fucked her and fingered her asshole, both of them grunting and moaning, chills running through her body as her orgasm approached like a runaway train.

But suddenly he pulled out, making her wail with frustration. She squeezed him with her thighs, wanting him back inside her, but he was dipping back into the jar of lube again and smearing it all over his cock.

"Oh God!" she whispered as she realized what he was going to do. He scooped up more of the lube and wiped it against her anus, and she looked at him with a mixture of astonishment, fear, and desire. She was frightened—she'd never done this before and yet she wanted it. It would be the ultimate assault on her, her total surrender.

He turned her over, and she started to raise her ass to him, but he slapped her down. She was surprised when he untied her wrists then rolled her over on her back again.

"Hold on to the headboard," he said. "And do as I say."

She did as she was told, lying on her back and gripping the metal headboard as he picked up her legs and pressed her knees back against her chest. She watched him as he looked down at his cock and she realized that he was going to take her from the front, hard and deep. She squealed as she felt the head of his cock searching through the smeared grease on her ass, looking for her tiny opening, and she jerked when he found it.

"Spread your ass, Vanessa. Spread your cheeks apart."

"Oh God! I can't!" she wailed.

"Do it!" he shouted, the look in his face scaring her.

She let go of the headboard and reached beneath herself and pulled her buttocks apart, squeezing her eyes shut as he guiding his cock to her anus and pressed forward.

Instinctively she clenched tight when she felt him there, and she could hear him panting and grunting with effort as he tried to fit the enormous head of his cock to her anus.

Somehow he managed to get the head past the tight ring of muscle and it popped inside her. He leaned all his weight against it and Vanessa felt herself give, trembling and shaking before his incredibly hard cock.

"No! Oh no!" she wailed, letting go of her ass and pressing against his chest, but he ignored her and continued to sink slowly into her ass, filling her with the most incredibly salacious feelings. Her mouth opened wide and a low, animal groan came out as he filled her belly with his shaft, plundering her most private place, shoving his cock into her very core.

She began panting from the pain, fast and shallow, taking a deep breath only to howl out her feeling of violation, and yet she loved it. She knew that this was the ultimate act, the most humiliating, most degrading. Truly she had reached bottom now, taking his cock up her ass like a slave. Her nipples were rock-hard with excitement, her pussy throbbed in sympathy and chills ran up her spine.

He was maybe halfway in when he stopped, gasping for breath, his eyes burning into her in her shame. He flexed his cock in her and she cried out again, he was so huge, so alive inside her. She didn't know what to do with her hands. They pushed at his hips to keep him out, then clawed at the bedspread, then covered her face. But he wasn't going to withdraw. She was going to get fucked in the ass, just as he'd promised, and her whole body trembled in terrified anticipation.

"Give me your hands." he said to her, flexing his cock again. "Hurry! Play with your pussy! Play with yourself, Vanessa. I want you to beat off while I take your ass!"

"Oh! Oh!" she couldn't even tell him no. She just let him put her hands on her empty pussy as he pulled his cock out a fraction of an inch and then pushed back into her, making her feel as if he were pushing her insides around. The feelings were so intense she hardly paid attention to what she was doing as she began to rub herself. But soon the pleasure of caressing herself lessened the pain of the anal invasion and replaced it with a terribly lewd and filthy pleasure that made all rational thought impossible.

He fucked her slowly, tentatively, pulling out and pushing in, feeding a bit more of his prick into her stretched ass with every stroke. His eyes were locked on her hands as she masturbated, and Vanessa gave a quavering moan as she realized that he was watching her so closely and that it was starting to feel good.

69

She found her clit with one hand and began to rub herself, her fingers brushing against his shaft just an inch or two below her. Her tongue came out and she licked her upper lip at the deliciously obscene feelings he was giving her, and then she started masturbating for real, egged on by the thought of what a total sleaze she had become.

He fucked her steadily but carefully now, studying her face in her agony of pleasure and shame as her masturbation became more and more frantic. The juice from her pussy poured down over his cock, lubricating it and easing his entrance further. She was alive all over, a mass of seething sensation in her ass and her sex, down her legs, her breasts, everything was on fire. Her hands found their rhythm as she rubbed herself, and soon they were working together, both of them driving her up that mountain from which there was only one way down.

Vanessa howled, her voice echoing off the bedroom walls and the family pictures. She couldn't tell whether she was coming or not, it had all merged into one unbearable hurricane of feelings. She was screaming constantly, yelling out and saying things she didn't even hear, begging him to fuck her hard, to ride her ass, telling him she was coming and urging him to come too, to join her in this frantic and impossible pleasure.

The tendons in her neck stood out as she raised her head to watch her fingers at her pussy and it suddenly hit her now what she had become, letting him fuck her ass while she masturbated for him, taking pleasure in her own degradation. Men had a word for a woman like her — many words, in fact — and as they played out in her brain and she felt the rich, evil thrill of them on her lips, she realized how far she had fallen and she exploded into fragments of shameless ecstasy, giving herself over to this salacious fucking, coming as she never had before.

She felt his cock throb inside her and then he was crying out and pumping his hot ejaculate into her ass, clawing at her, pulling her hair, making her take it as he shot again and again, scalding hot in her rectum. Vanessa's eyelids fluttered. She opened her mouth and extended her tongue as if she could taste him as he came. She beat on his body with her fists, urging it out of him, urging him to give it to her, and then she just seemed to go up and over, out of her body and into a black void of excruciating pleasure and pain, and consciousness itself dimmed and receded in the obliterating pleasure.

She was not out long, for she felt his deflated cock pull from her asshole trailing strings of his jism over her ass. She couldn't move. It was as if the muscles in her body just would not respond, and she lay there twitching and jerking in the aftermath of orgasm as Mr. Taylor took her in his arms and held her close in her helplessness, and she could feel him shuddering too from the intensity of his release. She was soaked with sweat, her hair matted to her face, and she felt sore all over—sore in places she'd never been sore before in her life, and yet she'd never felt so deeply satisfied, so totally used. He had hurled all his violent lust at her and she had taken all he'd given her and turned it into her own pleasure. No woman could have done more.

There was no use fighting the feeling—no use pretending that she didn't love it, being used and abused like this, and as he kissed her face and her shoulders, she took it as her due. She knew she would never be satisfied with anything less again.

Chapter Four

ॐ

It was a dingy and depressing city any time of day, but worse at night. The downtown was pockmarked with empty stores and abandoned buildings, and small bands of dangerous-looking boys stood on the corners in the semi-dark. It all made the hotel-casino seem that much more garish, looming up from the darkness and festooned with lights and chrome like a whore at a funeral.

The lights were welcome to Vanessa. The trip had taken almost two hours and for most of that time she'd been consumed by nervous guilt about the lies she'd told her mother. She tried to turn her guilt into anger directed against Mr. Taylor, but she wasn't having much luck. She'd already prepared her speech to him—the dramatic way she would tell him she was couldn't keep doing this, she wouldn't be his sex toy any more—she wouldn't keep lying to her mother and sneaking around. But unless she had anger behind it, she knew she wouldn't have a chance, and right now she was more excited than angry.

She worried, stared out at the lights and anxiously checked her cell phone again, waiting for that check-up call from her mother and rehearsing her lies—she was with her friends Ally and Jessica at Ally's dad's apartment, doing a little studying, but mostly taking a break, doing some shopping and getting their hair done, the kinds of things her mother was always pushing her to do by way of rest and relaxation just because Vanessa worked so hard.

The tour bus pulled into the circular drive, nonstop from the city to this rust-belt exurb casino in one hundred and fifteen minutes. Vanessa picked up her backpack from beneath the seat and took out her organizer to check the name once more, Mrs. Sneed Hearn III . That's who she was supposed to be.

She waited 'til the contingent of senior citizens had exited the bus then took the ring from her right hand, put it over the third finger of her left and turned it around so that the high school emblem wouldn't show. She grabbed her coat and followed them off.

It was cold out and as Vanessa waited for the driver to unload her bag, she looked around at the lights of the casino, flashing, spinning, racing toward the doors in an invitation to be sucked inside. Despite her misgivings about lying to her mother, the excitement was undeniable. She knew this was all hucksterism and hype, but still it was exciting.

A bellman took her suitcase and backpack and the doorman held the door for her. She felt a bit scruffy in her jeans and sweater and worn coat, but they didn't seem to mind.

Inside, the lights and noise hit her like a physical wave. There was an absurdly huge fountain commanding the middle of the room and reaching up some three stories into the air, and around it was the casino, a disorienting buzz of lights and racket after the quiet isolation of the bus. Clear glass elevators ran up the inside of the huge atrium, giving the place an unreal, science fiction feel, and around the edge of the casino were shops and restaurants and lounges, all open to the action on the casino floor.

Vanessa followed the bellman to the desk. "Mrs. Sneed Hearn," she told the clerk, trying to look adult. "My husband's already checked in."

She waited nervously, regretting once again that she hadn't dressed up a bit more. She felt positively shabby and worse, very young.

"Here you go, Mrs. Hearn, room 1718. Shall I have someone take your bags?"

"No, no," she said. She was worried about having to tip someone. Besides, the idea of someone else carrying her bags seemed just wrong to her. "I can manage, thanks."

Vanessa climbed into one of the chrome and glass elevators and pressed her floor. She accelerated upward from the sea of noise and people, and despite herself, she felt a surge of excitement—all the people, the cash and liquor and flesh, and somewhere out there was Rob, the man who was going to fuck her tonight and do the most outrageous and exciting things to her.

But no, she couldn't think like that. She knew she needed to confront him with the things she felt, it was making her crazy. She was already starting to waver and had been turning over the idea of just turning around and going back home. It wouldn't be that hard, and if he wanted to fire her for that, let him. The man had come into her life and made her his own sexual plaything, and now he maintained his power over her with the sheer force of his personality. She felt so overwhelmed by the emotions he caused within her.

There was nothing enjoyable or exciting about this, she told herself. She tried to summon her anger but in this glittering setting her anger wouldn't come.

A few people in the hallway glanced at her as they passed, and she tried to make herself small. She knew she looked like a schoolgirl. Maybe they'd believe she was someone's daughter or niece. Right. The old "niece" trick. Rob had used it before. This wasn't the first hotel trust he'd arranged for them, only the glitziest.

She knocked on the door, though Rob had told her he wouldn't be in. He'd be downstairs gambling. He said he'd leave her instructions in the room.

She used the key card. The lock clicked open and Vanessa stepped inside.

She stood and stared. The room was huge, a suite really— two floors connected by a sweeping chrome staircase. There was a sitting room in front of her with floor-to-ceiling windows that gave a view of the town and the lake and the skein of lights that ran along the highway back to the big city in the distance. The furniture was thick and substantial, the carpet absurdly deep, the television enormous. There was a bar and even a fireplace.

She walked to the window, dropped her bags on the big leather sofa and just stared at the view.

There was a note on the glass coffee table and she picked it up.

Vanessa — I've laid your things out for you in the bedroom. Dress in just what I've left for you and wait for me. I should be back about 9. — R.

Vanessa shucked off her coat and stepped out of her shoes, luxuriating in the lush carpeting beneath her feet. She already knew that Rob Taylor wasn't a piker — he always went first class, but this was something else — the whole nine yards. She walked around the suite, trailing her fingers across the furniture and playing with the dimmers for the lights. She found a panel on the mantel that controlled the fireplace, and when she turned a knob and pressed a button, gas flames ignited and began to glow warmly. She went behind the bar and got herself a bottle of water from the fridge, not caring what it cost.

This would be a great place for one of her fantasy games, she thought, absolutely perfect. With a growing warmth in her stomach, she realized that she didn't have to fantasize now. This was the real thing. She didn't have to pretend that there was a man who was going to dress her up and make her do forbidden and exciting things — he already existed. He was waiting for her downstairs. The thought gave her butterflies and made her nipples harden disconcertingly.

As if in reaction to her illicit excitement, she felt a sudden pang of guilt and remembered her mom and her promise to call. Vanessa still wasn't sure of what to say. She had hoped to maybe confront Taylor immediately and hit him with her

75

speech, then storm out, in which case she would have told her mother there'd been a change of plans and she was coming home. But now that she'd seen the suite and felt the excitement of the casino, she thought that maybe one night wouldn't be so bad. She could always come home tomorrow. She'd worked out a whole host of excuses for almost any possibility.

She got her cell and speed-dialed her number.

She talked to her mom as she sat on the sofa in the warmth of the gas fire with the lights of the city spread out before her. The lying was nerve-racking, but it wasn't as hard as she'd thought. After all, what choice did she have? She could hardly tell her mother the truth. She hung up quickly, saying she had to go, and then sat there holding the phone in her hand, wondering if she felt any different for lying. She didn't—not really—and she didn't know how she felt about that. She decided she'd think about it later.

She put down her water and walked up the curved staircase to the upper balcony. There was a bathroom at the end of the hallway, and she could see the gleam of pale marble inside. She walked over and turned on the light and smiled. The bathroom was enormous, almost the size of a little spa, with a huge tub sunk into the floor and a shower stall with multiple heads, big enough for a small party. There were two sinks, a toilet and a bidet, which she inspected with a little thrill in her stomach, imagining how it would feel to sit there and have the water play over her. How decadent!

The bedrooms were enormous, the beds proportionate. In the smaller of the two rooms she saw Taylor's bags, one on a luggage stand, the other on the bed. She looked at them for a moment then strolled over and opened one up. His clothes, mostly, but beneath that she found packages of women's things—bras and stockings, panties and gloves, all in their original packages and all her exact size. She opened the other suitcase, more of his clothes and beneath them a collection of sex toys and devices—vibrators, handcuffs, rope, leather cuffs. Her stomach tightened in nervous excitement.

76

She put everything back and zipped the bags closed. She went into the master bedroom.

It had everything—a table and chairs, a dresser, chest, two nightstands, a refrigerator, a huge walk-in closet and a dressing table with a large, round mirror. On the bed were two boxes—a shoebox from a very expensive store and a smaller, flat box, unmarked. She opened the shoebox first and found an elegant pair of silver-gray shoes with high, slim heels. Despite the size of the heels, the shoes weren't the sort of blatant, whorish thing she'd feared. He was always surprising her. On the one hand, he had impeccable taste for women's fashion, but on the other, he loved to dress her in the most outrageously lewd and suggestive outfits.

She pulled off her sock and slipped her foot into the shoe. Not bad. A bit snug, but the workmanship and comfort were impressive. All together not bad.

Wearing one heel and one cross-trainer, she sat down on the bed and opened the other box, the alarmingly small one. Inside was what looked like a tiny metallic ball gown for a four-year-old, and a barely-there black thong. Vanessa held the gown up by the shoulders to find that it was indeed a tiny dress made of some sort of metallic stretch fabric of bluish silver, with full-length sleeves and what looked like a fairly daring décolletage. Tentatively, she stretched it out, imagining how it would fit her. Even if she managed to get into it, she wouldn't have the nerve to leave the room. It would be skintight and much too short.

It was just eight. Vanessa took off her shoes and opened her suitcase. She took out some things and went into the enormous bathroom where she took a good, long, shower in the enormous stall, shaving herself all over as she knew he liked. She dried herself with a gorgeous towel taken from a warming rack, and found a brand-new complimentary terrycloth robe hanging on the back on the bathroom door. She wrapped the robe around her and thought that yes, she could get used to living like this, then went back to the bedroom and picked up the dress again.

No way. She could just imagine how short the thing would be. Even if the police didn't get her and she didn't die of absolute shame, men would be on her like flies on honey before she even got to the elevator. It was a whore dress. No. Worse than that—it was a porn star dress, or porn starlet, worn by some dumb little piece who didn't mind flaunting her silicon all over the place. Vanessa might let herself be talked into wearing it in the privacy of the suite, but never outside. She'd be safer in the nude.

"Vanessa?"

She heard his voice just before she heard the door slam. She started to respond and then caught herself. She wasn't about to go running to him like an excited puppy.

"Vanessa?"

"Up here," she called, trying to make her voice flat and blasé. She didn't want him walking around the suite bellowing her name, but she wasn't going to let him see her excitement.

She kept her eyes on the mirror and pretended to be busy brushing her hair as he came into the room carrying a parcel under his arm. Despite herself, she was impressed. Mr. Taylor was wearing a charcoal gray suit that looked very good on him. His eyes were shining with excitement from the liquor and gambling, and from finding her there in the suite after all. He really was a good-looking man.

She caught his eyes in the mirror and stopped with the brush in her hair. "If you think I'm wearing that thing outside of this room, you're crazy," she said.

He smiled but ignored her. "Wait 'til you see what else I've got," he said. "Look at this."

She'd been forced into coming here, and damned if she was going to look as if she were enjoying herself, but her curiosity got to her, and she turned around and watched as

Taylor opened the parcel. Inside was a box, and in the box a lot of Styrofoam peanuts that spilled out as he dug around inside.

"What is it?" she asked.

"Makeup. Morzhay cosmetics. They make the absolutely best stuff. Look."

He took out a plastic chest, skinned off the protective cellophane and opened it, and Vanessa saw it was filled with shades of eye shadow and blush. She'd seen collections like this before. They were either very cheap or ridiculously expensive. This one didn't look cheap.

Taylor looked at her critically, and then looked at the box, then back at her. He laughed.

"Fuck, I'm good," he said. "You're a Northern European twelve or thirteen. I knew it. Do I know skin tones? Like some men know baseball scores! Look."

He held up a small pallet of skin-tone blush next to her face. The colors were exactly the same as her complexion.

Vanessa looked at the little jewel-like pallets and remembered the speech she'd prepared. This was the man who'd walked into her house and intruded on her life, turned everything upside down and made her into his very own private sex toy. She tried to remind herself of that. God knew what new sexual perversions he had planned for her.

She thought about all this, and she said, "I didn't follow your instructions. I just couldn't, really. That dress, it's just too much. I couldn't go out in public like that. I just couldn't."

Taylor looked at her and smiled, a slightly dangerous, wicked smile, and at that moment Vanessa knew that there was more between them than just his lust. There was an understanding between them, a complementarity. Despite the difference in their age and background, despite the difference in who they were and how they came to be together, despite all of that, they were two parts of the same puzzle. What he wanted, she wanted—they fit together, positive and negative.

He looked at her. "Put it on," he said softly. It was half command, half plea and there was a note of urgency and desire in his voice that she'd forgotten about, a hunger that always excited her. "Put it on, Vanessa, but no looking in the mirror. I don't want you to see what you look like, not until I'm ready for it. Understand?"

She stared at him, fighting with herself. Despite her anger, something in his eagerness always overcame her resolve. He knew her too well. He knew what she liked. He was her perfect enabler, freeing her deepest desires. He allowed her to let go — no explanations, no apologies. With this man she could reach that part of herself.

Vanessa nodded. Yes, she understood. She understood completely.

Taylor put the box of makeup on the dressing table and then pulled the cover off the big bed. He threw the cover over the mirror on the dressing table.

"There," he said. "Now don't touch it and no peeking 'til I say."

Vanessa watched him, her excitement building. Her speech was forgotten. Her anger was forgotten. That familiar feeling of delicious anticipation began to build, the feeling she always got at the beginning of one of their sessions — the excitement before her transformation.

Since their relationship had begun, they'd developed a kind of sexual symbiosis, each one feeding off the other's excitement. He did the dressing and the designing, creating who she was going to be each session, and Vanessa was the subject, the model, the one who fell into each roll and lived it like it was her own. He was the dreamer, she was the dream, and no matter who she was, their sessions always ended with the same kind of intensely passionate sex as he reclaimed his creation and made her his.

So far all he'd done was play with her clothes, finding outfits for her to wear and dressing her, deciding who she was going to be, but he'd been talking about doing her makeup for weeks. Beauty was, after all, his profession, but they'd never had the time to really do it right before. It was too hard to arrange for an entire night, and their time together had always been counted in hours before she had to be home. Now that was all going to change. That was why he'd brought her here, and Vanessa was suddenly anxious to get started.

Taylor paused with his hand on the door and looked back at her. He saw the excitement already shining in her eyes. "Don't forget the thong," he said. "And remember—no peeking."

He didn't have to tell her. Vanessa knew exactly how the game was played.

The door closed behind him and she threw off the robe, tore the tags off the thong and quickly slipped it on, running it up her legs and snapping it into place over her shaved mons. It was the dress she wanted to get to, but the dress wasn't as easy. It was incredibly tight, and getting into it was like climbing through a rubber band, but finally she got the thing on over her head and breasts and, pulling and wiggling in a most unladylike manner, she brought it down over her naked body, feeling like a snake climbing back into a shed skin. Once she had pulled it down and gotten it as straight as she could get it, she smoothed it out and adjusted the neckline. She turned instinctively to the mirror.

The mirror was covered, of course, and so all she could do was check her sleeves and look down at herself over the hills of her breasts. The feel of the tight, slick material against her body told her all she needed to know. It was truly like a second skin—no, tighter, and with more support. It crushed her breasts like a lover's hands, lifted and molded her buttocks and stretched drumhead-tight against the muscles of her legs. She could feel where the hem caressed her thighs, no more than inches below her crotch.

Vanessa felt the blood rush to her face. She couldn't see herself but she knew she looked terribly sexy—devastating.

Taylor pushed the door open and just stood there looking at her, a gym bag in his hand. Vanessa looked up at him with something like feverish amazement, and for a moment their eyes were locked on each other's and they shared the thrill of conspirators. That's what they were, both of them conspiring to turn her into whatever he wanted her to be.

Taylor's mouth broadened into a wide grin. He laughed and shook his head. "Look at you! Better than I even thought. You feel it too, don't you, Vanessa?" He laughed again. "Yeah, I can tell. You feel it."

She was swept by a sudden wave of self-consciousness, but only for a moment. All she had to do was look into his face and her self-consciousness vanished. She knew that he saw her just as she felt. He was better than any mirror.

"Come here now, Vanessa. We're not finished. Come here and sit down. I'm going to do your face."

She didn't understand why he didn't just throw her down on the bed and take her just like that, because that's what the dress made her feel like. Instead he pulled out the chair from the dressing table and made her sit down. He quickly emptied out the box he'd brought, carefully arranging the makeup and bottles. He opened his gym bag and took out hair supplies— brushes and combs and clips, spray and mousse.

Vanessa looked at this collection in dumb wonder. She'd seen him operate on special clients in his shop where he had access to everything he needed, but now his efficiency and expertise amazed her. This man knew just what he was doing. It was like watching an artist.

He threw a towel around her shoulders to protect her dress then took off his jacket. He sat down opposite her and put his hands on her cheeks to hold her still as he studied her.

She felt nervous and aroused under his gaze and had to resist an urge to giggle. "What are you doing?"

"Hush. I've got a pretty good idea of what I want to do, but I want to make sure."

He turned her face this way and that, held her in profile, had her look up, look down. He stared at her as a diamond-cutter must look at a rare stone, weighing the options of where to strike to make it perfect. Vanessa was embarrassed. Really, it was terribly flattering to be studied like that. She knew she wasn't beautiful, not in the classical sense, not to her eyes. She had a good enough body, but her face was rather plain in her opinion. But not to Mr. Taylor. He saw things in her she never ever saw herself.

"What a face," he said as he turned her to the side yet again. "What a beautiful fucking face. You're just made for this, Vanessa."

She blushed, and his big grin made her blush even more.

He went to work on her hair, brushing it out, arranging it this way and that, trying it on top of her head or laying it over her eyes. In the end he brushed it all back close against her skull and clipped it in back, rolling the remainder into a little bun.

"Your face is a perfect oval," he said. "And the shape of your head is gorgeous. Not everyone can say that, so let's show it off. I don't want to hide you behind your hair. I want everyone's attention on this face."

No one had ever done her makeup for her before, not even in the shop, not since her pre-teen sleepover days, and it was terribly erotic now to feel the soft brushes and little sponges against her skin. She was the canvas on which he worked, and as he turned her face this way and that and brushed and blended her eye shadow Vanessa found herself growing very aroused. The dress was still holding her body in its tight, all-over embrace, the applicators licked at her cheeks and eyelids, and Taylor's face was inches from hers, his eyes intense. She was growing excited as she always did, and she felt that excitement as a need to be taken as he always took her, savagely, hungrily, almost against her will—to be pushed down and held there as his thick cock plundered between her legs.

83

The brushes teased and aroused, the feel of his eyes always on her made her wet and anxious, and the application of the makeup began to feel like a wicked and prolonged erotic torture, like foreplay.

She tried to concentrate on what he was doing. The colors he chose were not the colors she would have chosen, not at all, and she was afraid at one point that he must be all wrong in what he was doing, that maybe this was going to be some big, demeaning joke. But she didn't think his look of rapt concentration or the way his breathing deepened as he worked was fake, nor was the prominent bulge she noticed in his trousers, a sight that made her breath catch in her throat when she first saw it.

He finished with her lipstick and gloss, applying them with a brush, and the softness playing over her full lips was maddeningly arousing. She felt the sensuous glide of the brush in her nipples and her sex, like a lover's tongue on her mouth, and just when she thought she couldn't stand it anymore, he stopped and dropped the brush onto the table.

He stood up without a word and started putting his things away, capping the jars and cleaning off his brushes. He looked at her once more, turning her face from side to side, then he stood up. He took her by the hand and had her stand too, then pulled the bed cover off the mirror with a dramatic flourish.

The breath caught in her throat. She was beautiful, so beautiful that the sight of her own reflection made her nipples harden in desire. She was flawless, perfect—somewhere between a face and a mask, and light-years away from her college student persona. He hadn't used too much makeup as she'd feared, and the colors he'd chosen and the subtlety he'd used made her face into a jewel. Her eyes were large and dramatic without looking cheap, her lips were full and expectant. Her expression, with her features relaxed like this, was one of sensual tranquility and slight hauteur.

And then there was the dress. Vanessa knew all about sexy clothes, from the cute to the blatantly whorish, but she couldn't decide where this one belonged. The metallic fabric was painted on her body—she looked like she was made out of chrome, like a sculpture. Her breasts were shiny hemispheres, the arch of her rib cage and the ripples of her abdominal muscles were accented in gleaming highlights, and where the liquid flash of the dress ended, the perfect creamy tan of her naked thighs began.

It might have all seemed too cheap if it weren't for the regal beauty of her face. The severity of her hair pulled back tightly against her head gave the entire package a kind of superhuman look, as if she were not quite of this world.

Taylor didn't even look at her as she studied herself, leaning toward the mirror to see how he'd blended her eye shadow. He went into the bathroom and washed his hands, then came back into the room and picked up his jacket.

"Well?" he asked.

Vanessa was speechless. She'd gone from being a shy and scruffy college girl into a sort of archetype of feminine beauty, and her feelings were a jumble of confusion—a vague feeling of insult, as if she herself weren't good enough, and yet a terrible thrill of power at the sight of her own unexpected beauty, and all combined with a kind of chagrin that he'd managed to find this beauty inside her. Taylor had reached a place deep down inside her and found someone new, someone she hadn't even known existed. *Power* was the word that best described what she felt. It left her breathless.

"It's incredible," she said. "I mean, I've seen some of the girls you did in the shop, but they were models…"

She saw his smile as he slipped casually into his jacket and picked up her shoes. He walked up behind her and peered over her shoulder into the mirror, his eyes catching hers. "What have I been telling you, Vanessa? Why do you always think I'm bullshitting you?"

She couldn't answer, and he laughed with delight,

"Well, Miss Mechanical Engineer," he dropped the shoes at her feet. "What do you think of yourself now?"

Vanessa didn't know how to answer. She looked back into the mirror and said, "I don't even recognize myself. I look so different, so much...older."

"No," he said. "Not older. *Beautiful*. That's the word. You're fucking beautiful."

He reached into his pocket and pulled out a jewelry box and took out a set of earrings and a necklace. "Here," he said. "Not the real thing, but they'll do."

The earrings were shimmering strands of rhinestone. The necklace was white gold with purplish-blue amethysts that echoed the dress's cool blue highlights, surrounding a polished cabochon of amber. The amber's warmth was a relief against the perfect, almost frigid beauty he'd created. Like everything else, the jewelry he'd picked out for her was just perfect. She was no longer surprised at his tastes.

"Are you ready?" he asked.

"Ready? For what?" She looked at him in horror. "I'm not going out like this."

He didn't argue. "I didn't spend all this time and money to get you dressed up so that you could sit inside and get your rocks off posing in the mirror and playing with yourself. This is the real world now, Vanessa. This isn't a game. This is who you are. We're going to take you out and show you off. And that's not all."

Taylor reached into another pocket and pulled out a small velvet bag. Vanessa watched as he reached inside and pulled out a small plastic egg—a vibrator, cordless, with a small wire hanging from one end. He held it up by the wire like a dead mouse.

He smiled. "Remote control. A range of about 60 feet."

Her eyes went wide when she realized what he wanted her to do. "Oh no," she said. "Absolutely not."

"There's some lube in the bathroom," he said. "Get in there and put it in. I've got the controller right in my pocket. Fresh batteries, all set to go."

"No!" Vanessa said as he grabbed her by the arm and dragged her down the hallway. "No. This dress is bad enough. I'm not going to wear that thing!"

"Come on, Vanessa! We've come too far for this bullshit. You won't be the only one dressed to kill out there. Only the most gorgeous. Now get in there and put that thing in and enough fucking around."

He pushed her into the bathroom and closed the door, and Vanessa stood there uncertainly for a moment, fuming at him. He always did this—just when she was starting to feel her own prowess, he managed to take the upper hand—stealing the rush she was beginning to enjoy.

She looked at herself in the mirror, marveling again at this unexpected beauty. She knew what he had planned for her. He was going to take her into the casino and any time he wanted he would hit the switch and send waves of pleasure radiating through her body, right there in public. He'd control her like a puppet on a string, and people all around would see her trying to fight off her humiliating arousal, see her maybe gripping his arm and trying to stifle her moans as she orgasmed right there at one of the gambling tables.

She had a sudden image of herself there—head thrown back, red lips parted, all eyes on her as she got her secret sleazy pleasure. Everyone would see what she was. What a devastatingly beautiful tramp. She felt chills on her neck and a hungry warmth between her legs.

Vanessa hiked her skirt up and sat on the toilet. She pulled her thong to the side and slid the egg into her vagina, already so wet that it went in with no trouble whatsoever. She replaced the thong, the tight fabric closing her labia around it so snugly that just the soft little antennae hung out of her. She tucked it up under the thong.

"Let's see," Taylor said as she emerged from the bathroom. He boldly reached under her dress and ran his fingers over the thong as Vanessa was forced to stand there like a piece of property. It was demeaning and humiliating, but the feel of his fingers on her pussy almost made her groan out loud. They hadn't even left the room yet and already she was dying for him.

Taylor found the antennae wire where it passed over her clit and smiled. "You hot little tease! You're already wet, aren't you? And now for a little test."

He reached in his pocket and hit the controller. Vanessa gasped as the thing jumped inside her and began thrumming away. It wasn't pleasure. It was more like being violated, and yet that feeling of being intimately touched in so callous and mechanical a manner was exciting in itself. She would be totally under his control, and that was terribly arousing in itself, though she would die before she admitted that. She grabbed onto his arm and dug her nails in, fighting to maintain her composure.

Taylor switched it off, smiling with pleasure.

"Please," she gasped. "Go easy on me, Rob. Please."

He smiled. "You just do what I say, Vanessa, and everything will be fine."

He handed her a little clutch bag done in the same fabric as the dress, and together they descended the suite's impressive staircase. He waited for her as she threw a few things into the bag, though her hands were shaking and she was hardly thinking clearly. Taylor led her from the suite, the door closing behind them with a solid click.

At once Vanessa was aware of the unfamiliar weight and fullness of the vibrator inside her as she walked. She felt the coolness of the air on her bare thighs and wafting up beneath the tiny skirt where the panty clung tightly to her privates, holding the wicked egg in place. The thong insinuated itself between her buttocks, working against her anus as she walked.

She looked like a piece of chrome and she felt like a loaded pistol, cocked and ready to go off at any time.

Chapter Five

ഇ

They rode down in silence 'til a loud foursome got on the elevator at the eleventh floor. They took one look at Vanessa and their conversation ebbed away, stumbled and stopped. Vanessa felt her face grow hot with embarrassment, but Taylor stood there beaming happily, pleased with the effect she had on these people. She felt uneasy but strangely triumphant as well. She stood erect, looking coolly out at the lobby as it approached and they descended into the swirl of activity. Despite her embarrassment, she felt like she was descending from heaven to the world of mortals.

Taylor led her from the elevator and across the carpet, and again Vanessa felt eyes turning in her direction. One part of her mind wanted to yell out that she was not what she seemed — only a college girl, forced to dress up in this outrageous outfit — but another part of her basked in the attention and dared any man to look at her as she passed. She wasn't sure what she was anymore.

Taylor didn't go to the blackjack or poker tables where the serious gamblers were, but to roulette and craps, where he could stand in a crowd and make it obvious that this beauty was with him. He didn't talk much to her, nor she to him. She knew instinctively what her role was, and despite herself, she found it strangely exciting. She was there to be admired, like a painting or a precious stone, and it occurred to her that the stereotype of the dumb, silent blonde might be terribly mistaken. Maybe these women were smarter than they looked and knew instinctively that they weren't there for their powers of conversation. Maybe speaking or any sign of intelligence just ruined the effect of supernatural beauty.

90

She watched him gamble, but all the time she was aware of the silent vibrator waiting in her vagina, sitting there like a ticking time bomb, and she couldn't follow the play. She saw enough to know that his luck wasn't good, but she found it impossible to concentrate or take part in the excitement. The wickedly high heels made her stand on tiptoe, her back swayed, ass out and shoulders back, breasts thrust out, totally conscious of the vibrator inside her and of the controller waiting patiently in Taylor's pocket. She was aware that men were looking at her—women too—but all she could think about was the little egg and the way it bound her to him. Taylor's control was as complete as if she'd had an iron collar around her neck and she kept close to him, afraid to let him out of her sight.

Drinks started arriving and Vanessa helped herself, spurred on by her own nervousness. The thought of what he could do to her in front of all these people had her tense and wet and she drained the first two drinks too quickly, before she realized she had to slow down. She hadn't eaten for hours and she was never much of a drinker. The liquor went right to her head. The casino was a blaze of flashing lights and mirrors, and every time Vanessa caught sight of herself she felt a little thrill of shame and excitement. Her hands were shaking with nervousness.

Taylor started winning, and eventually she was caught up in the action—chips flying, people shouting and laughing, the tense roll of the dice and explosions of sound when the numbers came up. By the time he handed her two rolls of silver dollars and said, "Go play the slots, Vanessa, I've got a good feeling for you," she'd all but forgotten about the little vibrator and almost felt at home in these clothes.

The dress hugged her ass and moved enticingly against her naked buttocks as she walked over to the bank of machines. She could feel men's eyes on her and wondered whether she'd ever get used to it or whether she even liked it. The machines distracted her. She liked the feel of feeding the heavy coins into the silver slot and the satisfying resistance of the massive lever, the solid chunk of the reels as the fruit and bars fell into place. Just as he'd predicted, on her fourth coin she won as three oranges thumped into place and the machine exploded with lights and racket. An avalanche of silver dollars spilled noisily into the tray and Vanessa buzzed with a little surge of adrenaline.

She was just bending over to sweep the coins into her hand when there was a sudden explosion of sensation between her legs as the vibrator leapt to life. Vanessa grabbed onto the tray of the machine with both hands and bit her lip to keep from crying out as the thing buzzed inside her. There was pleasure to it now, a deep, shameful stimulation of her secret spots. It lasted only a few seconds and then stopped, leaving her thighs weak and her nipples erect and throbbing.

She looked up to see Taylor smiling at her from the craps table ten paces away, his hand nonchalantly stuffed into his jacket pocket. He hit the switch again and another wild hum exploded deep inside her in a kind of sexual earthquake. She felt her pussy spasm and close on the vibrator as if trying to draw it into herself.

"Give you a hand, miss?"

She looked up to see a young man standing at her elbow, his blond hair falling casually over one eye, his model's chin perfectly shaded by the right amount of stubble. He was too handsome—almost pretty—though he couldn't have been much older than Vanessa. Still, under the circumstances this was not what she needed. There was something predatory about him.

"No, I...I just need something to hold all this change in."

He reached atop a nearby machine, brought down a cardboard bucket and smiled at her.

"It's not fair that a lady should be so gorgeous *and* so lucky," he said with a smile. "There ought to be a law. Here, allow me."

He took one of the silver dollars and fed it back into the slot machine and nodded for her to pull again. Trapped between the stranger and the machine, Vanessa pulled the lever again just as Taylor hit the buzzer and the vibrator exploded in her pussy. It hit her hard, and she hung on the lever as waves of lewd, disembodied sexual pleasure licked at her body.

Dimly she heard the mechanism engage and the wheels spin. Her thighs were trembling along with the vibrator as she clenched her eyes shut and bit her lip, tasting her own lip gloss. She tried to control herself—the stranger was standing right at her elbow—but despite her efforts a shuddering gasp passed through her lips. The first reel clunked into place and the vibrations ceased.

Vanessa held absolutely still as the other two reels jerked into place—a blank, a plum, a bar. No winner. She was red with shame as she turned her head and glared over her shoulder at Taylor, standing twenty feet away, a grin on his face.

"Wow," the man said, his eyes growing hot. "I like the way you play. You really get into it. Come on, try again. My dollar."

"No I—"

He reached past her and dropped a coin in the slot. Vanessa hung on the lever, not daring to move, and the man covered her hand with his, softly closed his fingers over hers and pulled. The reels spun and his hand lingered on hers a bit too long.

Again the vibrator jumped and began to buzz inside her sheath. She gasped and held on fiercely to the cold chromed handle. The antennae wire had come loose and hummed against her clit and Vanessa felt like her entire lower body was turning into fiery liquid.

"Oh God! Oh fuck!" she whispered hotly, her eyes closed and teeth clenched as she pressed her forehead against the cold machine. Her thighs were shaking and she couldn't help but press her mound against the counter, squeezing her buttocks tight in a vain attempt to make the buzzing stop.

"Christ!" the man whispered, pushing his body against hers. "You're one hot little piece, you know that, baby? You really get off on this gambling, don't you?"

The buzzing stopped and Vanessa almost fell. She held onto the lever of the slot machine and twisted away from him. She looked at him in confusion, trying to see through the mist of lust that clouded her sight.

"I'm sorry," she gasped. "I'm not well."

The man smiled wickedly. "Come on, baby. I don't know what's going on, but let's play it again." He put his arm around her shoulders and fed another dollar into the slot.

And then Taylor was there, insinuating himself between them and taking Vanessa by the arms. "Excuse me, friend," he said. "The lady's spoken for. She's a bit under the weather, I'm afraid, and she really shouldn't be out"

A few people looked around and Vanessa felt herself blush bright red. The aftershocks of the vibrator were still echoing inside her and her legs felt weak and watery.

"And who asked you?" the man said. He was taller than Rob but thinner and younger. He wasn't going to move.

Taylor took the bucket of her winnings and gave it to a drink girl along with two twenties. "Take this to the cashier, honey. Have him send the receipt to room 1718. Mr. and Mrs. Sneed Hearn III."

He turned back to the glowering man and smiled at him, his grin as bright and cold as ice, then took Vanessa by the arm and pulled her from the machine. The crowd parted and the man gave ground. Vanessa stumbled after him, eager to get away from the people's stares. She walked as fast as she could, given the sudden weakness in her legs.

"You bastard!" she said when she'd caught her breath. "You son of a bitch!"

94

"Come on." He grinned as he steered her along through the crowd with his hand in the small of her back. "How about a dance, Vanessa? Wouldn't that be nice?"

There were restaurants and bars right on the edges of the casino floor, open to the gambling area to encourage easy come and go, and in one a band was playing and people dancing. It was dark, there was a bar and the music was from another era—big band swing, rich and brassy. The dancers were mostly older, retirement-home types.

"What are you doing?" she demanded. "I don't know how to dance to this stuff."

"Yeah. Me neither. No problem though. Watch."

He took her hand and led her back into the crowd, away from the casino where the man still stood glaring after them. Once they were blocked by the crowd of oldsters Taylor turned her to face him, took her right hand in his left and put his other arm around her waist. He pulled her close and Vanessa instinctively put her hand on his shoulder as she'd learned back in social dancing.

"Rob, I've got to sit down. My legs are weak and I can't stand up in these heels."

"Mr. Taylor," he corrected. "I like when you call me Mr. Taylor. I like the formality. Now just follow me. It's easy."

His hand slid down to the small of her back and pressed her against him. She could feel his erection through his slacks.

She was afraid to move her feet, afraid she'd step on his foot with her sharp heels and make a fool of herself, but fortunately, moving her feet wasn't necessary. Taylor's version of dancing didn't involve any motion below the knees. He just held her and swayed to the music, pressing himself against her and making her stomach jerk with subliminal excitement as she felt his erection press against her lower belly with animal urgency.

95

Even in her heels she was below his eye level, so she couldn't see what he was looking at as he let go of her waist and his hand went to his pocket.

"Oh God!" she moaned, instinctively tightening her grip on him. "Don't! Please!"

There were people all around them shuffling to the music, oldsters mostly, but some younger couples too. The vibrations turned her into melted butter and she dug her nails into the back of his neck to hold on as her legs started shaking again. Taylor left the vibrator running and reached around and grabbed her ass through the sheer metallic dress and pulled her close. He could feel the vibrations through her body, throbbing through her pubic bone and buzzing against his cock where it was pressed against her and the thought of her with that vibrator inside of her—the realization that she might be on the verge of orgasm here on this crowded dance floor drove him wild.

"Oh God! Oh God!" Vanessa moaned, trying to hide her face against his chest. Her hips shoved hard at him of their own accord, her buttocks clenching as she pushed her mound at him, seeking some relief from the maddening throbbing in her swollen channel.

Taylor held her tight and whispered in her ear. "Look at all these people here, Vanessa, all of them seeing what a tramp you are. You're going to come, aren't you? Are you going to come right here in front of everybody and show them what you are?"

The vibrations were rolling through her pussy, the little antenna sawing against her engorged clit like a violin bow. She was all liquid between her stomach and her knees, except where Taylor's fingers dug into her ass, holding her up. His hard cock lay like a bar of iron against her belly and Vanessa pushed hard against him as if she could impale herself on it even through her clothes.

He killed the switch and the vibrations stopped, but Vanessa clung to him, unable to let him go. She could still feel the echo of the vibrations inside and she needed the solidity of his body against hers. She knew she should hate him and the way he made a spectacle of her, but instead she felt more wildly attracted to him than ever. The way he used her and controlled her was more erotic and arousing than she could have dreamed. She hung on him, anticipating and dreading the next jolt.

The band hit a little crescendo and Taylor swung her around like a dance hall Lothario. Vanessa just got her heels beneath her and regained her balance when he hit the switch again and again the deep, fast throbbing rocked her to the core, but this time she was ready for it and she clamped down on the vibrating egg as if trying it draw it deeper inside. Taylor had her in a dark corner and his hand slid beneath the back of her short skirt and cupped her naked buttock. His finger worked its way beneath the thong and pressed against her anus, forcing her groin against his hard shaft. Vanessa growled like a cat in heat and pressed hard against him, then opened her mouth and bit his chest through his shirt, out of her mind with lust.

"Christ!" he snarled. His own excitement fed off hers. He raised his hand and brought it down hard on her naked buttock. The sound was masked by the band, but he felt the spank jolt through her body and Vanessa squealed.

"Come for me, Vanessa! Come for me right here where everyone can see you!"

Great waves of obliterating pleasure rolled through her pelvis as she shoved her pussy hard against him. Her legs were shaking again and she was tempted to let go and let it happen. Taylor's finger pushed into her rectum and Vanessa threw her arms around his neck and held him tight, crushing her breasts against him. Her buttocks clenched as she humped against his stiff rod and her lips sought his mouth, eager to hide herself in a kiss.

Time seemed to stand still as she pressed against him, marked only by the deep, insistent throbbing that pushed her up and up, up to where she'd have no choice but to surrender to him and let go, climaxing in his arms.

At the critical moment, just when she thought she couldn't possibly stop it, the band suddenly ended the tune, the trumpets standing up to sound their loud, raucous chord, and Taylor reached reluctantly into his pocket and turned off the switch.

Vanessa moaned in anguish and frustration, unwilling to come back down off the edge of sexual climax. Her body was swollen and aroused, her pussy throbbing. Her dress seemed extra tight and as thin as cellophane, so sheer and unsubstantial that she felt like anyone could see through it and see the sex-mad woman within. Her thong was soaked. She could feel her own lubrication slicking the insides of her thighs as Taylor steered her out off the dance floor and out to the cashier's cage where he cashed in all his chips for neatly packaged stacks of bills. The cashier slid over his income tax report form, then Taylor took Vanessa's arm and steered her toward the elevators.

She walked in front of him in a daze, chest thrust out as though she were the figurehead on the prow of a ship, cleaving a path through a sea of people. She was dizzy and throbbing with need, bursting with sexual energy, and again her feelings toward Taylor had taken a confusing change of direction. There was no question of telling him off and defying him now. All she wanted was to be taken and used as he always used her — fucked, held down and stuffed full of cock — taken with that savagery that thrilled her so much and was so unlike anything she'd ever known with anyone else.

Her helpless arousal might be a product of the vibrating egg still inside her, but there was something more subtle and consuming going on as well — the feeling of being so absolutely controlled, of being used and turned into whatever he wanted her to be. She had come a long way with Rob Taylor since that evening in her mother's kitchen and she was no longer the girl she had known back then. Dressed as she was tonight, she was his creation, designed, built and operated by and for Mr. Robert Taylor. She owed herself to him and only he knew all the different sides of her. Only he could give her what she needed.

The elevator started up and Taylor hit the switch in his pocket again and pulled her to him. Vanessa felt the dizzying acceleration of the elevator and the wild hum of the vibrator at the same time. She no longer fought against the maddening sensations but gave herself over to them and let them run through her as if he were already having her. She locked her hands around his neck and let herself melt against him, shoving her humming groin hard against his hip, not caring that they could be seen by the people on the floor below. The elevator was fast. Vanessa whimpered as she clung to him and ground her thrumming pussy urgently against his cock. She slid the fingers of one hand inside his shirt, desperate to feel his skin, and he left it on, tormenting her 'til they reached their floor.

They staggered out of the elevator, a passing couple smiling knowingly at one another as they passed, thinking Vanessa was drunk and that's the way she walked, hanging onto him, weak with sexual starvation.

Inside the suite she could scarcely contain her impatience as Taylor emptied his pockets onto the table. Vanessa leaned on a chair and watched him—keys, stacks of bills, a few uncashed chips. The cash gave a thrilling, illicit air to what they were doing, as if she weren't already aroused enough.

Her sessions with Mr. Taylor always had a definite structure. First he would force her to dress in whatever kind of clothes he'd brought, then he'd parade her around as the clothes worked their magic on her, getting her hot and aroused. Then the sex would start—lewd, thrilling, sometimes even degrading sex, the reward and punishment for her behavior—and sex that satisfied Vanessa beyond all reason.

But now things were different. They weren't just playing in his living room. They were away together and the clothes weren't just a temporary costume—they were who she was. Taylor had made her over into someone new. He'd taken her out in public, confirming this new identity and cementing it in place. Vanessa was a creature entirely of his making now and she loved it. Every fantasy she had ever had, every stolen moment alone of dress-up in her bedroom, he had made real.

Taylor looked up at her as he finished emptying his pockets. The last thing he pulled out was the little white plastic controller. He stared right at Vanessa and turned it on.

"Oh fuck!" she gasped, her nails digging into the padded back of a chair for support.

There was no reason to hold back any longer. She was alone with him in this suite and no one would know. Vanessa hung her head and moaned. She reached down beneath her legs and pressed her fingers against herself, desperate for the sensation, not caring that he saw. She had to come. She needed the release. Her nerves were raw.

"Not so fast." Taylor turned off the vibe and went to the switch that controlled the curtains. He pressed a button and they slid back, revealing the lights of the city below, gleaming like diamonds spread out in the black velvet night.

By focusing her eyes right, Vanessa could see their own reflections in the dark glass too, a dim mirror image floating in the darkness over the city—this forbiddingly beautiful woman and the man who had made her.

He came up to her and took her in his arms and Vanessa threw her hands around his neck, ready and eager to give herself. His lips came down on hers and she kissed him greedily, sucking his tongue into her mouth, her breath racing through her nostrils.

"Please," she whispered as their lips parted. "Fuck me. Please, Rob. I'm begging you. I need it."

Taylor smiled. "You're so fucking gorgeous. Who would have ever thought?"

He laughed, ran his hands down her back and squeezed her buttocks again and Vanessa felt herself melt.

"Just stay there," he said.

He trotted upstairs and came out of the bedroom carrying his suitcase, the one she'd looked through earlier. Vanessa watched as he took out a length of sturdy rope and tied it to one of the balusters of the second-floor rail, then let the free end dangle down close to where she stood. He came downstairs and laid the suitcase on the table, opened it and took out a pair of black leather cuffs set with silver buckles and rings.

Vanessa wasn't surprised. She'd seen all his gear when she'd looked through his suitcase before and she knew of his particular tastes and now she was too excited and needy to object when he buckled the cuffs on her wrists and made her his prisoner. All she asked was, "Are these really necessary?"

"Yes," he said, cinching up the second one. "Yes they are."

He got up and retrieved some hardware from the suitcase. He seemed to have this all planned out and he quickly clipped her wrists together and tied another piece of rope to them. He tied a loop in the hanging rope then passed the line from her cuffs through it and by pulling on the other end, he raised her hands inexorably over her head.

She let him do whatever he wanted to her, wincing only when he pulled so hard he threatened to pull her off her feet. Her need was so great that if this is what it took, she was willing.

She stood with her wrists together, her arms stretched over her head, just balancing on her spike heels. The position of her arms lifted the hem of the dress so that it just covered her crotch. She could feel the air on her damp thong. The vibrator was still inside her.

Taylor finished tying her off and ran his hands down her arms, admiring the lines of her body. He smiled and walked around her slowly, gazing at her from all angles.

"You really are beautiful," he said. "An untouchable beauty, too lovely for any man. How does that feel, Vanessa?"

She didn't answer. She was pulsing, throbbing from her previous excitement, and her helplessness now only added to her consuming need. Her breathing was quick and shallow — she was almost panting like an animal — and raised her breasts with every breath. Taylor watched her for a while then went to the suitcase and took out a slim riding crop, perhaps two feet long. Vanessa felt her stomach tighten and her wetness increase. Yes. She was ready for it. She wanted it.

"I imagine it must feel lonely," he said. "A little forbidding. To be so good-looking that you even intimidate people? Is that how it is, Vanessa?"

He reached out and ran the crop up between her breasts then down around each one, tracing a lazy spiral that ran inward 'til it circled her stiff nipples. Vanessa closed her eyes. It felt frightening and terribly good.

"I would imagine that such beauty even involves a kind of guilt. To provoke so much lust in men, and women too. I'd imagine such beauty might even seek out some punishment as a way for atoning for itself."

"I don't know," she said dully, hardly understanding what he was saying, just wanting him to get on with it. "I don't know what you're talking about. What are you going to do?"

He brought the whip back and slapped it sharply against Vanessa's nipple, making her gasp as a little flash of pain shot down her arm. He slapped the other breast and Vanessa gasped again. Despite her distress, she felt her nipples harden.

"This is what I mean," he said. "A little whipping, a little training."

102

He slapped her again and her nipples, already achingly hard seemed to sit up and beg like trained dogs, wanting more, betraying her

He came around in front of her and ran his hand over her helpless body, from her bound wrist, down her arm, over her armpit and around to her heavy breast, which he squeezed so hard she groaned again, then down over her ribs, her side, her hip. The metallic dress was as slick and tight as silver paint, but the warm resilience of her flesh beneath it made his blood pound in his veins.

He moved around behind her and she heard the whip slice through the air before it landed on the thin fabric covering her buttocks, sending a ripping pain across her ass and a spear of fire through her loins. He hit her again, then again, then put the crop under his arm and worked the snug hem of her dress up over her hips, uncovering her naked ass. She could feel the welts as he caressed her buttocks. She could sense him smiling behind her.

He came around in front of her and took hold of the neckline of the dress. He peeled it slowly out and down, exposing her naked breasts, then let it slip back into place beneath them, the stretchy fabric pushing her breasts up and together in a sumptuous cleavage, presenting them like two ripe peaches on a silver platter. Her nipples were erect, the red patches from the whip still visible.

Smackk!!

The whip came down again on her stiff little peak and Vanessa threw her head back in pain—a luscious pain, deep and sexual.

Whapp!!

He hit the other nipple and she closed her eyes tight so she wouldn't have to see.

That was all, though, and the next blow was on the inside of her trembling thigh. She braced herself and the next blow hit her right between her legs. Vanessa felt the hot splash of the whip in her dripping pool of her sex. She whimpered and tried instinctively to lower her arms to protect her sensitive breasts, but of course she couldn't. She was helpless before him, totally defenseless.

Taylor changed his tactic, bringing the whip up from the bottom of each breast in a series of brief, pattering slaps that made Vanessa suck in her belly as the spears of pleasure-pain became too intense. Her thong was just soaked now, the juice was streaming from her.

"Beautiful," Taylor said, walking to the table. "So beautiful it hurts. Did you know that, Vanessa? Did you know that men hurt when they look at a woman as beautiful as you? That you can cause them physical pain?"

He picked up the controller and slipped it into his pants pocket and Vanessa kept her eyes glued to him as he approached.

"You know what a man wants to do with a woman as beautiful as you? He wants to bring her down to his level. He wants to make her want it as much as he does. He wants to punish her."

She was expecting it, so when he hit the switch it didn't surprise her, but still the sensations were overwhelming and Vanessa grabbed the rope so tight she almost pulled herself off the floor. He dialed down the controller so instead of the sharp electric buzzes she'd received in the casino, it was now seducing her with a deep, slow throbbing, almost like the rhythm of sex itself. She felt her sheath grab at it in a greedy spasm and then the slow throbbing spread to every corner of her body, setting her on fire. She let her head fall back and she wailed, beyond shame, beyond embarrassment.

The whip came down on her exposed ass again and Vanessa cried out. He whipped her again and yet again, the slim shaft slapping against her innocent behind as the vibrator throbbed and pulsed inside her, turning the fiery pain into deep, vicious pleasure.

The thought occurred to her that she should protest, make him stop, or at least turn away and protect herself, but tied and half-naked in this expensive suite, already aching for sexual punishment, she took it as her due. It felt right somehow, as if she deserved it, as if she had to pay for her beauty.

Vanessa threw her head back and opened her mouth to the ceiling, giving herself over completely to the dual sensations ravaging her body—the obscene, insistent thrum of the vibrator inside her and the sharp ferocious sting of the leather whip on her ass. Her thighs trembled and her breasts heaved above the confines of her dress. She didn't even try to fight it any longer. She wanted it. She welcomed it.

"Oh God!" she wailed. "I'm going to come! I can't stop it! I'm going to come!"

Taylor threw down the whip. He seized her from behind, crushed her body to his and dug his fingers into her sex, pushing the thong aside to expose her naked flesh. He pushed two fingers into her and felt the plastic egg buzzing away. He found the antennae wire where it hung from her, seized it and slowly—very slowly—pulled the buzzing device out of her.

"Ahhh! Oh God! Yes! Yes!"

Vanessa climaxed just as the egg was halfway out of her, poised at her entrance where she was most sensitive. The powerful vibrations made his fingers hum as they pressed against her and she just exploded into great, racking spasms that snapped her body like a whip, her breasts trembling, thighs quivering. She lost all strength and slumped helplessly in the rope and Taylor held her up, one hand between her legs, the other clamped so tightly on her breast that the flesh bulged between his fingers as if it would burst.

Vanessa went limp, her head falling back against his shoulder as she felt the orgasmic pleasure just pour out of her body as if she were being squeezed like a sponge. The man utterly controlled her and she was helpless to do anything but stand in the rope and feel just what he wanted her to feel. He pulled the egg all the way out and dropped it to the floor, where it lay buzzing and quivering on the plush carpet.

Taylor hit the switch, then turned it off and slowly the shattering waves of pleasure she felt subsided as well. Strength returned to her legs and as her mind cleared she was aware that she'd let herself go too far. She'd allowed herself be his slave and the shocking power of her orgasm showed that she'd loved every minute of it.

Vanessa shuddered all over, a whole-body spasm that arose not only from her deep, abject satisfaction but from the knowledge that things had changed between them. The vibrator and his fingers had made her come, but the whipping was what had given her climax its savage edge. She'd loved it and they both knew it. All she could do now was wait to see what Taylor would do about it.

He reached up and unclipped her wrists from the stretched rope. The bulge in the front of his pants was ludicrous, but Vanessa wasn't laughing as he untied her from the rope and unclipped her wrists.

"Take it off," he said, and Vanessa was seized by a sudden, inexplicable nervousness. As long as she wore the dress, she wasn't herself, but his creation. Once she took it off and stood naked before him…

"Come on. Off!" He picked up the crop and gave her a little slap on her red and beaten ass. "We both know what's what now, Vanessa. So get the dress off. I'm not done with you yet."

She peeled the tight dress off her body and let it fall to the floor. He tapped the crop against her thong and Vanessa took that off too, holding onto the rope for balance. She was dressed now only in her shoes and jewelry, and even though the room was dim, she could still see herself in the mirror behind the bar, her hair swept back, her makeup still perfect. The body was hers, the face was still someone else's, though someone she was getting to know very well.

Her legs were weaker than she'd thought and she wobbled slightly in her heels as he led her over to the sofa. Taylor took her wrists and clipped them together in front of her.

"Kneel," he said, indicating the sofa.

Vanessa got down with her knees on the cushion, her forearms resting on the back. The sofa faced into the room, so kneeling like this Vanessa was facing out, presenting her ass to him and looking right out the big glass windows and the fairyland lights of the city below. She could also see her reflection in the window and Taylor standing behind her, opening his belt and pulling down his zipper.

Her heart began to hammer in her chest. He was going to fuck her now and she was ashamed at how much she wanted it, his big cock moving inside her, taking what was his. No matter how much she hated him or detested what he did, when she felt him inside her and possessing her, she was totally his, free of all guilt and shame, free to feel everything he did to her. It had been like that from the start.

She looked at their reflections again, her breasts hanging below her, her earrings flashing light. Taylor's shirt was off and now he pulled the belt from his pants and doubled it over in his hand. Vanessa gasped in fear and bit her lip, waiting for the blow.

"You love it, don't you?" he asked her as he dragged the cool leather over her buttocks. "You love playing the tease, making me want you. You loved everything I did to you tonight, didn't you?"

She didn't dare answer. She saw him draw his hand back and then the belt slapped down on her sore bottom and Vanessa sobbed with deep, masochistic pleasure — a pleasure she could hardly understand. It stung, it burned and it kindled the fire inside her again. She could feel her whole body throb with every blow. She dug her nails into the back of the sofa and hung on.

She deserved it. She deserved it because she was beautiful and because she made him want her so much. She deserved it because she wanted him to fuck her and do terrible and obscene things to her. She deserved it because she needed to know how much he wanted her and because she knew he wanted her to the point of pain. She deserved it because she wanted to feel everything that was his—she had absolutely no use for herself anymore.

Taylor worked himself into a frenzy. She could hear him grunting and swearing behind her as he whipped her, even after her ass went numb so there was nothing left but this deep, hot, liquid feel between her legs. He threw the belt aside and she felt the cushion sag as he knelt behind her on the sofa. She sobbed again and dropped her head when he fit the rock-hard tip of his cock against her flooded pussy and then shoved savagely inside her.

"Oh! Oh God!" she cried. She looked up to see the reflection of her own beautiful face in the dark window, her features contorted into a mask of obscene lust as Taylor took her from behind like an animal, thrusting into her like a demented bull. His angry passion thrilled her and Vanessa took it as her due. She hung on to the back of the sofa as Taylor bent over her and shoved deep into her young body, making her take it and showing her no mercy.

"Just like this," he snarled down at her. "Like two animals. That's what you are, isn't it, Vanessa? A hot little animal masquerading as a lady. Getting all dressed up and parading that hot ass around like butter wouldn't melt in your mouth and all the time you're wet between your legs, thinking of a big hard cock reaming you out."

"Oh God, yes!" she screamed through clenched teeth. "Just fuck me! Fuck me hard!"

His loins slapped against her ass, her tits swung up and back and the heavy sofa began to inch across the carpet from the brutal force of his thrusts. Vanessa felt herself building to another climax, pushed upward by his savage lust. She felt the fires building again, that obliterating haze gathering. All she could think about was the feel of his hard male tool pistoning in and out of her, making her love it.

"No!" she cried when she suddenly felt him pull out of her, leaving her alone and stranded, hanging on the edge of release, her ass cocked lewdly up into the air.

Taylor got off the sofa and went quickly to the suitcase, rummaged around and came back with a small jar. Vanessa put her cheek down on her bound wrists and groaned.

"Yes, baby. Let's do it like this," Taylor said as he smeared the lube around her puckered asshole. "All my life I've been waiting for something like you. To take a girl and turn her into my idea of beauty, make her drop-dead gorgeous. Make her so hot she makes me hard just to look at her. Make her perfect and then get her alone and take control of her. Make her do everything I want. Make her mine."

Vanessa yelped as he slid two fingers into her ass. She put her head down, her back hollowing as she waited for the pain to ebb, because she knew it would. It wasn't the first time he'd taken her there and though she'd never told him, he must have known how much she'd loved it.

"Oh fuck!" she moaned as he slathered more grease all over his cock and knelt behind her, pushing his cock head against her rectum. "Take it slow, please, Mr. Taylor. Please..."

He pushed. He put his big hands on her buttocks and spread them apart so he could watch the head of his cock stretching her out and sinking slowly into her. She could hear his breath hissing through his teeth and she was no better, whimpering and pleading for him to go slow. She felt like she was being ripped in half as he stretched her but she was young and her body adjusted, and soon she felt his entire length slithering into her rectum. It was a thrill like no other—totally owned, totally dominated, totally possessed.

"Oh my God! Oh fuck!" she moaned hotly as her body quaked with erotic seizures, trembling on the very edge of orgasmic release. Taylor reached under her and found her nipples. He seized them and pinched savagely, making her squeal with abject pain and savage delight.

"Who owns you, Vanessa? Who fucking owns you?"

"You do, Mr. Taylor. You always do! Oh God! Only you!"

She looked up at their reflection in the window and saw herself bent over in slavish obeisance. Taylor loomed over her like some pagan god, his chest swollen with male power and arousal. He fucked her steadily now, his cock sliding back and forth in her slippery bottom like a piston in a sleeve, fucking her so hard that her long, dangling earrings began to swing, shooting sparkles of light against the walls and carpet.

Vanessa moaned. She hummed and she crooned with pleasure. She looked at her reflection and thought, *What a beauty I am! What a beauty and what a slut! All I ever wanted to be!* She felt Taylor's fingers dig into her hips, felt him harden and thicken inside her, felt the sudden savagery of his lust as he reached for his completion, then heard his harsh bellow of triumph as he finished inside her.

Vanessa put her face down and bit the edge of the sofa to stifle her own screams as her orgasm surged beneath her like a ocean wave, carrying her up, up and over and then down into a realm of obscene and glittering darkness.

It was so good. It was so terrifyingly good.

Chapter Six

ഇ

She awoke in the gray dawn at a bleary six a.m., her class-day habits not affected by the night of debauchery or the smeared and smudged makeup she still wore. She extracted herself from beneath Rob's body and made her way to the bathroom where she showered and washed away all vestiges of last night. As always after a session with him, she felt a nagging guilt, and she scrubbed herself 'til she was pink and almost raw. She dried her hair, brushed it out and fixed it behind her head in a severe ponytail. She brushed her teeth and looked at herself in the mirror as if she would see someone else there.

She dressed and threw her things into her backpack and took out a pen and a piece of paper for a note. The shuttles ran back and forth to the city every hour round the clock and she'd be gone before he ever woke up. He had planned on their making a day of it and he no doubt had more fun and games planned, but Vanessa had had enough. Last night had frightened her, had touched her to her core and she needed to get away. She was so scared of the way he made her feel—so out of control—distance was the only salvation she could come up with. Maybe if she could put some space between them, then she could think straight. She stood at the table with the paper before her and tried to think of what to write.

The evidence of last night's debauchery was all around her—the rope hanging from the stairs, the crop and the vibrator, the jar of lube still on the table. She was surprised that the sight of these things didn't nauseate her, but she felt emotionally neutral. She had been someone else last night—someone not quite herself, but someone she knew quite well and someone she couldn't quite hold responsible, but still, she wasn't her now and she had to get away. She remembered the way the men and women in the casino had looked at her and she remembered the look in Mr. Taylor's eyes as well.

She wrote on the paper:

I'm catching the early bus back to the city. I can't do this anymore and I've decided I really don't want to see you again. Please don't call.

Vanessa

She let herself out and took the elevator down to the main floor, gray and deserted and tired at this hour, despite all the flashing lights and artificial gaiety. She checked on the bus departure time, then went into the snack shop and ordered a bagel and coffee. She was suddenly ravenous.

She had just added cream to her coffee and opened her textbook to the chapter she should have read days ago when someone approached her.

"Hey there! Feeling better this morning?"

Vanessa looked up and saw the man from the slot machines last night, a suitcase in his hand. In the light of day he didn't seem so predatory, just remarkably handsome with a model's natural grace and a bit of easy arrogance that wasn't unattractive. He was dressed smartly, in a leather coat and dark glasses.

Vanessa felt embarrassed. Morning wasn't her best time and she was dressed in her scruffy student clothes without any makeup. She was surprised he recognized her.

"Oh hi. Yes. Yes, it was just some little bug or something. I'm fine now."

He glanced at the seat opposite her. "Waiting for your friend?"

She felt herself blush, remembering all that had happened last night.

"Oh no, no. I'm not staying. I've got to get back. Got classes." She pointed to the open textbook in front of her.

Feeling she had to explain herself, she added, "He's just an old friend. He's staying on for a few days and I just came down to visit, but I've got to get back. Waiting for the bus."

"The bus? Oh that's too bad." He smiled and indicated the empty seat. "May I?"

She smiled and shrugged her approval. Anyone who was an enemy of Rob's seemed like an ally to her and this young man was much closer to her in age, maybe someone she could relate to. She wasn't above a little company, a little protection.

"So you're a student, I see. What are you studying?"

Vanessa blushed. "Mechanical engineering."

"Oh wow!" He laughed. "Way over my head. I quit after high school. That was more than enough for me." He put out his hand. "I'm Brian Ackerman."

"Vanessa Wallace."

He looked at her appraisingly until Vanessa felt uneasy. Then he laughed.

"Sorry," he said. "Don't tell me you're shy. But you look so different than you did last night. I think I like you better like this. You're really quite beautiful, Vanessa. You've got the bones, the structure."

Before she could react, he disarmed her nervousness with a little laugh. "I notice that kind of thing. I'm in the business. I do male modeling. Maybe you recognize me?"

Now that he mentioned it, he did look rather familiar, but it was his type—thin without being skinny, with a classically handsome face and arresting green eyes.

"Bouret watches, Henri Cru men's wear? I did some stuff for Cutting Edge too, but that was two years ago. The Christmas catalog. Hot corduroy for a cold season?"

Vanessa shrugged then smiled. She didn't want him to think she was unfriendly. She was glad of the company.

"I'm getting more into the production end of it though," he said. "Modeling is such a cut-throat business and too demanding. You've either got an eating disorder, or you're out of work, did you know that? The women especially. Next time you're envying some model in an ad, think of her on her knees puking her guts out in the crapper because she had a piece of chocolate last night. That should put it into perspective for you."

Vanessa laughed uneasily. "I never thought of it that way."

"You ever consider it?" he asked, tilting his head. "Modeling, I mean. You've got the figure for it and the face. It's not all really as bad as I made it out to be. There's a lot of money in it and we're always looking for new faces."

He reached into his jacket pocket and pulled out a card case, extracted a business card and handed it to her. It said "Brian Ackerman Productions, Ltd.". In the background was a cityscape.

"You've got beautiful hands too. That's how I started out, as a hand model." He showed her his hands, running the fingers of one over the back of the other as if he were showing off gloves. It was a slightly effeminate gesture that made her strangely uneasy.

Brian laughed. "It's a weird business. Weirder than mechanical engineering. But it pays better too."

He called the waitress over and ordered juice and tea and that was all. Vanessa felt ashamed of her bagel and cream cheese. He noticed and laughed. "You should eat what you want. It looks good on you. For me it's just habit."

He told her about his business, what he did and how he did it—screening model applicants and picking and choosing, arranging for their publicity shots, shopping them around, getting publicity for his agency and drumming up business. He was doing well, had fifteen models right now and was expanding from advertising work into trade shows and live fashion work. By the time they were finished drinking coffee the bus had come and gone. Brian would drive her back in his shiny new SUV. It was a long way from the bus—warm, dark and smelling of leather. Vanessa knew the music he played and the bands he mentioned. As they waited to pay a toll he turned to her.

"May I ask you something? Take your hair out of that ponytail and shake it free."

Vanessa laughed, but it was fun to play. Her times with Rob fed this empowerment she now felt—the awareness of her sexuality. She did as he said, shaking her head 'til her hair fell in her face.

Brian didn't laugh. "You need a trim," he said. "It's a little long in the back. You go to a guy I know and he'll take care of you and then we'll get some shots taken, no charge. What do you say? Doesn't cost you anything."

"Brian, I don't want to be a model."

"Fair enough. Then how about you just agree to wear some clothes and stand around and I'll give you three hundred dollars an hour?"

"Three hundred dollars an hour? Is that what they make?"

"For a start? Yeah, around there, give or take another couple hundred."

He paid the toll and they zoomed away, Brian raising his window as they went.

"You've got something, Vanessa. You don't look like a model. You look like just what you are, a college kid, and I'm willing to bet you'll clean up real good. Now all I'm asking is that you get a haircut on me and give me a few hours of your time for some promo pics and let me see what I can do. What do you say?"

"You're serious?" She laughed in disbelief. "That's all I have to do?"

He smiled. "That's all, baby. Is it a deal?"

Three hundred dollars was just a little less than what she'd made in a week doing Mr. Taylor's books and now, if she quit that job, that source of income was gone.

"What kind of haircut?" she asked, and Brian smiled.

* * * * *

The hair stylists were good. Expensive too. Their shop was downtown, right off Michigan Avenue, and all she had to do was mention Brian's name and they were falling all over themselves to get her into a chair, fawning over her, playing with her hair, discussing her. She knew the hair stylist Mr. Taylor used, an aging queen known as Randolph who would sit and look at a girl's face for what seemed like hours as he smoked one cigarette after another before he even picked up scissors and they were nothing like that. They turned her this way and that, picked up her hair and let it fall. They argued and fought. They talked about lift and drape and fall and camera shadow and Vanessa felt like a queen.

Finally they called in Fulgencio to add some color. Aubergine, he said. Chestnut wouldn't do. Then Gene cut her, or *shaped* her rather.

Brian came back and watched them work, but the only comment made was toward the end, when he told her to look at him like she was going to take him to the bedroom, her most seductive look. Vanessa felt silly, but the three hairdressers all came and stood by Brian as she lowered her face and looked at them from beneath her lashes, giving them what she hoped was a suitably seductive look.

Brian nodded. He was satisfied. He handed Gene an envelope of cash and then led Vanessa into a corner. He took out another envelope.

"Here's three hundred dollars. I want you to meet me at this photographer's tomorrow about ten o'clock," he said, turning and writing an address on the envelope. "And I want you looking good. Most of my girls dress down on the street so that's not a problem, but not as far down as you, Vanessa. Go over to Wolverton's and get yourself some clothes, some sharp jeans, a nice top, classy. This photographer's a friend of mine. I want you to look good when you come in."

She should have been embarrassed, but she wasn't. Brian was right. With her new haircut, her clothes looked like rags. She looked almost impoverished and she felt all wrong. She took the money and put it in her pocket.

"Okay, Brian. I guess I do look kind of grubby."

He smiled and kissed her on the forehead, winked at her and walked out.

They hadn't done much to her hair, but they'd done something and men looked at her as she crossed the street and she felt it bounce against her neck. She went into Wolverton's and lost herself in looking at clothes for a while. They weren't the kinds of things Brian wanted her to buy and they weren't the kinds of things she ever could have afforded before. But now, with the salary he promised her, they were within her grasp and Vanessa was entranced. As she browsed, she saw other young women—slim, in jeans and sunglasses—and she realized that they might be models too. That's how they dressed. She picked up their style effortlessly and in a few minutes she'd picked out just what she thought he wanted—a pair of jeans that fit her beautifully and a rust-colored sweater that picked out the new highlights in her hair. She paid cash and the sales girl was very deferential. Vanessa realized that she took her for a model as well. She skipped across the street and headed for home.

She got home as the phone was ringing. She looked at the caller ID and saw it was him—Rob Taylor. She knew this was coming, but now with her new haircut and her new confidence she thought this might be the time.

"Hello?"

"Vanessa? It's me, Rob. Uh, listen, I saw your note..."

"Yes, Mr. Taylor. Rob. It's over. We're done."

117

He was silent for a minute. "Well, look, if I went too far last night... Is that it? You didn't get off on it?"

She got control of herself and said, "No. It's nothing like that. I've just had enough. I don't want to do it anymore."

He was quiet for a moment then said. "You're sure. See, I thought we had an understanding..."

"Understanding?" she said incredulously. "Oh sure. You dress me up and encourage me to express my sexuality whenever you feel like it and in return I give in to you and tell lies to cover it up. No, Mr. Taylor, that's not the kind of understanding I want with anyone."

"Vanessa, look, I'm sorry. If there's some way I can make it up to you, anything I can do—"

"Yes there is," she said suddenly. "Leave me alone. And find a new bookkeeper, I quit. I've met someone else. Someone who thinks I'm better than the things you use me for. Brian Ackerman. He owns a modeling agency. He wants me to work for him."

"Ackerman?" Taylor sounded doubtful. "I don't know any Ackerman. Vanessa, listen, be careful what you're getting into. There's some bad characters out there."

She laughed bitterly. "You don't have to tell me about that, Mr. Taylor. Believe me, you don't."

"Well, what kind of modeling? I know most of the fashion agencies and they—"

"Why don't you take it up with him now? He's handling my business. You can reach me through him."

"Vanessa—"

"Brian Ackerman Productions, Limited. You can look him up. Goodbye, Mr. Taylor. *Rob.*"

She hung up the phone and stood there, ringing with the feeling of new-found freedom. She only had to turn to the hall mirror to see herself and her new haircut—her confidence and maturity. She reached in her pocket and took out the envelope and checked the address of the photographer. A decent neighborhood. She went to the hall closet and pulled down the phonebook and looked up Brian's agency and there it was, a quarter page spread. She already had the number memorized.

She realized her mother would be home soon and she was thankful she'd given her the excuse she had—that she'd been staying downtown with friends and doing some shopping. That would explain her haircut and even her new clothes.

Her clothes! Vanessa took the packages and trotted up the stairs and opened them, then jumped into the shower. She washed, got into her underwear and slipped into the new jeans and sweater.

Yes, she could feel the quality, the fit. She could get used to this. She liked the way she looked.

She pulled out her books and got to work on the homework she should have done last night, but more than once as she pondered a problem she found herself caressing her new clothes, running her hands down the snug fit of the denim over her thighs, or feeling the way the knit of the sweater hung from her breasts.

Yes, she could get used to this.

Chapter Seven

ဢ

She did look sharp when she walked into the studio the next morning in her new clothes and a pair of not-too-scandalous boots that Mr. Taylor had bought her. She looked just right, in fact, casual and effortlessly elegant, and she felt the part—like a model. She had thrown some old clothes and her best makeup into her backpack because she thought that was what other models did too and it gave her a casual, don't-give-a-damn look she wanted to achieve.

It was just Brian and the photographer in the studio—Gino McCall—a short, swarthy man with a shaved head and a goatee who moved around sleepily in flip-flops and a bathrobe, yawning and drinking coffee from an enormous mug.

The studio was hardly impressive but just what she'd expected of a hard-working photographer—a loft above a printing plant with a small, dismal reception area lined with blow-ups of magazine covers by Gino McCall, none of them very new, and though she wanted to be impressed, she had the distinct impression of a man whose biggest successes were behind him now. Inside it was respectable enough and bigger than she'd expected, all lights and cables and camera equipment, backdrops and racks of clothes. Vanessa glanced at the clothes but wouldn't let herself look too closely, afraid she might start to stare and fall into what Mr. Taylor had called her "spells", though it seemed to her that Gino and Brian exchanged a quick, surreptitious look when they saw her interest.

She couldn't really tell what Gino thought of her, as sleepy as he was, but Brian gave her a little lift of his eyebrows to show her she looked good, even though she wasn't dressed or fully made up yet. He led her to a dressing room in the back.

"You need help with your makeup?" Brian asked her. "Bonnie isn't coming in 'til one. That's Gino's girl, but you can handle it yourself, right?"

"How long will this take, Brian? I've got a class at one."

"A class? Oh right. We'll be done by then and if it runs over, no big deal, you miss a class. You're going to make scads more money as a model than as a chemical engineer."

"Mechanical engineer," she corrected.

He laughed. "Whatever. Just get your face on. Nothing too much. Want you youthful and pure-looking, but a little seductive, you know? Jennifer Co-ed, but she's available. That kind of thing? Shiny lips?"

"What am I going to be wearing? What color? Warm or cool or…"

"Whatever," he said again. "You know, like here." He opened a lingerie catalog for her and pointed to a model, all legs and tits and cheekbones with glossy, blowjob lips—classic male fantasy stuff. Apparently Brian wasn't as sophisticated with his makeup as Mr. Taylor had been. Vanessa looked at the size of the girl's breasts with some concern.

"Okay," she said. "I'll do my best."

"Good. Don't take too long. We've got a lot to do."

Vanessa had learned a lot from Rob Taylor and he'd bought her some very good cosmetics. She tucked a towel around her neck to protect her sweater then set about putting on a face that wasn't as extreme as the model Brian wanted her to emulate but far beyond anything she would ever wear on campus.

She had trouble with her hair though and was a little miffed that there was no one there to help her brush it out and arrange it. It had looked so good after the cut, but now it didn't seem to hang right. She fluffed it out as best she could and walked out.

Gino had a chair and camera set up in one corner of the studio and Vanessa was disappointed that she wasn't going to be center stage under the big lights, but Brian explained these were just head shots at first, just for publicity.

Gino sat her down and posed her—this way, that way. He tossed her hair around a bit then started shooting, one shot after another, a cigarette in his mouth. He kept the camera on the tripod and had her move in the chair—turning her head this way and that, spinning around, shoulder up, down—and Vanessa thought that kind of odd—not just the way he posed her, but his general disinterest.

"That was great," Brian said. "That'll give us more than enough for your book."

"My book?"

"Yeah. You know, your portfolio, the pictures we send around to other agencies and photographers."

Gino was fooling with the camera. "She's got to sign the releases."

"Oh yeah."

Brian walked over to a cluttered table and combed through some piles of paper then brought some forms over. "You've got to sign the releases so we can use the shots. Standard stuff. Just here. And here. And once more, right here. Great."

Vanessa signed and then stood there uncertainly while Gino went to get more coffee.

"Is that it?" she asked.

"Oh no, no," Brian said, folding the papers and putting them in his pocket. "Now we take some with the sweater off."

"What?"

Brian looked at her as if it was obvious. "Just take the sweater off, baby. No big deal. We want to see your chest and shoulders, your bone structure."

Gino came back with a fresh mug of coffee, stirring it with his finger. He seemed bored.

"Come on, Vanessa," Brian said, "Don't be silly. You want to be a model? The clients want to see the body they're hiring. Hold your sweater in front of your boobs if you're so embarrassed about it."

He was probably right, she thought, but she wasn't certain. Gino looked at her with something between boredom and contempt. She had the distinct feeling he had more important things to do. Brian sighed and walked over to her and took her arm, leading her away from Gino so he could speak low.

"Look, Vanessa, don't embarrass me, okay? This is how it's done. McCall's one of the best and he's doing this for me as a favor, but it's still costing me plenty and the longer you piddle around, the more it costs, understand? Believe me, we've seen more tits than we can count and no one's going to jump on you."

He walked away and Vanessa thought it over then angrily pulled her sweater up over her head. She'd done worse than this and if they wanted to see her body, then they could damn well see her body.

Gino took a couple of pictures of her back and front and Vanessa dropped her sweater and stood there in her bra. Gino looked up from the camera and made a flat face as if to say he wasn't seeing anything special. "Maybe we want to put her in the Diana bra. Maybe that would help."

"Good idea." Brian went to a rack and searched through it, pulling down a lacey black bra. "Try this on and we'll see how you look."

Vanessa took the garment and stared at it. She recognized the label—a mid-quality manufacturer known for erotic lingerie and sexy playwear and the model was designed to enhance a woman's cleavage. It wasn't much of a garment and she'd never considered herself especially well-endowed, but both men seemed to expect her to put it on. Gino looked bored and Brian a little impatient, so she went into the changing room and took off her bra and put on the new one. It was her size exactly, but it was padded and the fit was strange. The padding irritated her, like she wasn't good enough. She had to play with her boobs to get it right and when she seemed to have it adjusted she found it lifted her breasts and pushed them together very suggestively.

She looked in the mirror. She did look better. It excited her, she couldn't deny it, but she felt something else too, something like anger. This was all getting very much like Mr. Taylor, only without the look of lust in his eye. When she walked out of the changing room, the two men were looking at her like a piece of meat.

"Let's do the whole outfit," Brian said.

He handed her another hanger with a sheer wrap on it and a tiny thong panty. The phone rang in the studio and Gino went to answer it and now she noticed that his robe was open and he was only wearing shorts underneath—boxer shorts, it looked like. He stood there talking about business, idly scratching his stomach, and Vanessa stood there bewildered. It was all such a strange mixture of sexuality and normalcy—a business. Posing, showing herself—it was like selling soup.

She went back in and tore the labels off the panties and slipped them on and couldn't help thinking of standing in front of the mirror in her bedroom playing her game. She let them snap into place and smoothed them out, then turned around and looked at her rear in the mirror. The panties were tight and sheer, they stretched tight across her buttocks, showing her crack as an enticingly shadowy valley. That thrill came back, the thrill of her own sexuality. She couldn't deny it.

The peignoir seemed silly. She didn't even know women wore things like this anymore, then she realized that no one wore anything like this anymore—it was all for effect. It was cheesecake.

She slipped into her shoes and walked out and Brian lifted his brows in approval when he saw her. Gino was leaning against a counter, blowing streams of smoke at the ceiling. His robe had fallen open and he was indeed wearing boxer shorts, and hideous ones at that, with some sort of pattern on them. He didn't seem the least bit self-conscious about it.

"Turn around, sweetheart," Brian said.

Vanessa turned a circle, holding her arms out, and saw the two men exchange glances.

Gino crushed his cigarette out and stepped up to the camera. "Well, she's got nice abs and a good ass. Legs are okay too, but I don't think she has the white meat on top. That's what sells."

"It's good enough," Brian said. "We'll use a cup size too small and a little padding and she'll be spilling out. And that's a gorgeous ass. She'll look great in silk, with some higher heels."

Gino shrugged and Vanessa felt herself redden. The men looked at her like a race horse or heat of cattle and for the first time she missed seeing the fire she used to see in Mr. Taylor's eyes when he looked at her. She'd been good enough for him, and he was one of the best.

"Besides," Brian said, "it's that face I love. That innocence."

Gino looked through the camera and said, "She needs more color if you ask me. She's too plain, too blah. Looks like she wouldn't know one end of a dick from the other. A little girl playing dress-up."

It went on like that, one outfit after another, an entire collection of lingerie and "playwear", each one worse and more suggestive than the other. Brian was mildly enthusiastic, Gino was totally unimpressed. She wore stockings, camisoles and teddies, opera gloves and leather slave collars. They put her hair up and took it down and in between shots, stung by Gino's comments, Vanessa kept on adding to her makeup, putting on more, trying to emulate the catalog picture Brian had shown her, but it was all no good. She couldn't get into it, couldn't let the clothes take her over.

She missed the heat she felt with Rob, that look in his eyes. Even when he did the most terrible and outrageous things to her, there was never any doubt about the depth of his feeling for her, the look in his eyes, the reverent way he touched her. With these two men she was just tits and ass and the clothes were just clothes. Whatever they wanted from her, she knew she wasn't giving it to them.

Her last outfit was a corset that Brian laced tight, forcing her breasts up and out and compressing her waist so that she could scarcely breathe. She wore long, seamed stockings with Cuban heels, velvet opera gloves and a matching choker set with a silver ring and they posed her with a whip. Gino pulled the card from the camera and wrote on it with a marker and said, "I think that's enough. It's not going to get any better. Sorry, sweetheart."

Vanessa was close to tears. All morning she'd been stripping and dressing and posing until she hardly felt human anymore. She'd completely missed her class and Gino's regular staff was starting to shuffle into the studio, still sleepy at one p.m. No one gave her more than a glance.

Brian came over and took her arm. "That's great, honey. Why don't you go get dressed now while me and Gino have a talk."

Vanessa knew they were going to be evaluating her photos now and she knew the results wouldn't be good. "He hates me, doesn't he? He thinks I'm worthless."

"Honey, Gino's kind of eccentric. He sees a lot of women, an awful lot, and he's got peculiar tastes. He's an artist and he doesn't know what the public wants, what sells. You get dressed and meet me in that office over there in five minutes, okay? And don't cry. Take off some of that eye makeup. You'll get it on your sweater."

"And oh yeah," he added, "that Diana bra you tried on? The first one? Wear it now, okay? It's yours. I want you to wear it now, under this sweater, understand?"

"But why?"

"Just do it!" he said, his eyes suddenly hard. Clearly, some strain was getting to him too.

He forced a smile and made his eyes kind. "Do it for me. Give us five minutes, then come on in and we'll discuss it."

Vanessa watched as Gino gathered up the memory cards and he and Brian walked into the office, then she went in the changing room and tore off the clothes. She knew she'd failed the test and that's what this had been—an audition before the camera and the camera hadn't liked her.

As she sat there undoing the corset, a woman came by, a frumpy, middle-aged woman who could only be Bonnie, Gino's makeup woman. She stood there squinting at Vanessa through the smoke of her cigarette.

"You shouldn't wear so much eyeliner, sugar. Makes you look like a mime."

Vanessa pulled on her jeans and her boots then searched through the pile of clothes for the Diana bra. She put it on and adjusted her boobs, then slipped on her sweater. The bra raised her breasts and made her feel gratifyingly cheap and aggressive, like her breasts were weapons. Some aides were already straightening up the dressing room as she got her things and left and she realized that Brian had hired the studio in its off hours, probably saving money that way.

She walked to the office and knocked, anger and shame making a lump in her chest. Gino opened the door and she walked into a dark room lit by the flicker of four computer screens. Brian sat in a big leather chair behind a desk and Gino, still wearing his robe and boxers, lounged against the wall behind him. Vanessa recognized herself on the screens, but as she looked at them she realized those hadn't been the outfits she'd been wearing. The colors had been changed, some details had been added. They'd been playing with her images, enhancing them with a computer program and she found that slightly offensive.

"How much do you want this job, Vanessa?" Brian asked. He was slouched down in the big chair playing with a letter opener, his face impassive, looking as powerful as a studio executive.

Vanessa didn't know what to say.

"I can offer you six hundred dollars for one night a week to start, that's two hours of work, cash money. If things work out, there'll be more."

She looked at Gino, who didn't seem contemptuous anymore, only slightly amused as he waited for her answer. Brian's offer had caught her totally off guard.

"Three hundred dollars an hour?" she asked. "What do I have to do?"

Brian tossed the letter opener on the desk.

"Pretty much what you did here today. Model lingerie in front of people. Put it on, walk around, come backstage and take it off and put something else on. Standard fashion show stuff."

"Oh Brian! Really? I did okay then?"

"You were marginal, dear, marginal. That's why I have to know how much you want it."

"Yes, I want it. That would be great!"

"Good," he said. "And you'll be willing to work for it?"

"Of course," she said. "What else do I have to do?"

He gestured with his chin. "Get down on your knees."

"What?"

Gino laughed.

"Don't mind him," Brian said. "I'm not going to touch you. Just do what I said. Take off your sweater and get down on your knees. Over here, by me."

She watched in horrified fascination as Brian opened his trousers and pulled down the zipper, hooked his thumbs into the waistband of his shorts then stopped, looking at her.

"Well?" he asked.

She walked around to the side of the desk, feeling a strange sense of power in this scenario, and Brian lifted his hips and slid his pants and shorts down his legs. His cock was hard.

"We sell lingerie," he said, loosening his tie and unbuttoning his shirt. "There's just one test I use for a model's suitability. That she look good enough to get me off. The sweater, please. Take it off."

Gino folded his arms over his chest and leaned back, a smug look on his face as if he had bet Brian she wouldn't do it, but it was becoming automatic to her now, and Vanessa lifted the sweater over her head and threw it onto a chair, standing there in the special bra that made her tits look so good.

"I could almost get hard off that belly," Gino said. "She's got a killer stomach."

"Gino's gay," Brian said, pushing his shirt back off his chest so he wouldn't soil it. "Or bi, or whatever the flavor of the week is." He smiled, taking his cock in his hand and starting to stroke it. "There's extra bonus points if you get him off, but I wouldn't worry about that. Now get on your knees."

"Brian—"

"I told you I'm not going to touch you and you're not going to touch me. I just have to look at you. Strictly business."

"Brian—"

"I might have to come on you though. If you're very, very good. Now on your knees."

Vanessa held onto the desk and got on her knees, a foot, two feet from where Brian sat with his legs apart, his cock erect now as he pumped it. His eyes went from her face to her breasts, then back up at her and she realized he was looking for the reaction in her eyes to the sight of his masturbating for her, as if that should be enough to get a reaction from her.

"You know what they say about a man's hands and his cock?" he asked softly. "It's true. Beautiful hands, beautiful cock. It is beautiful, isn't it? Probably the most beautiful cock you've ever seen. That's why no one touches it but me. So don't even think of it."

Vanessa knelt with her hands on her thighs, not certain what to do. He did have a handsome cock, straight and elegant as a Grecian column and quite large, but the aesthetics of his penis were the last things on her mind right now. His balls rolled lazily as he stroked himself and she felt this lewd, sinking feeling in her stomach, a breathless expectancy.

"Oh yes," Brian said softly as he masturbated. "I can see her on the runway right now, with those young tits and high ass. Men go crazy for young stuff. I can see her strutting around and her ass jiggling just the right amount. We'll have to get her some good shoes and teach her how to walk, but I can see it. Can't you, Gino? Every dick in the place hard?"

Gino cleared his throat and, glancing over, Vanessa saw his cock was hard too and emerging through the fly in his shorts, short and thick, but his eyes seemed more on Brian's hand than on Vanessa and now she could form some idea of the strange relationship between these men — Brian finding the girls and bringing them to Gino, who photographed them so that he could watch Brian masturbate.

Her tight jeans were pressing against her crotch and she was starting to throb from the mere salaciousness of what she was doing, which was nothing more than providing the fodder for Brian's masturbation. The skimpy bra left the tops of her breasts exposed and she could almost feel the heat from his tool on her skin.

She had no desire for Brian. She didn't even like him, but he was a terribly beautiful man and with his shirt open and spread back he had the body and face of a Greek sculpture, muscular and virile — too pretty to be true. He had no compunction about showing the ecstasy on his face as he pleasured himself either and his very self-absorption and selfish pleasure was a strange kind of turn-on. Vanessa stared at his cock with hypnotic fixation as his hand moved up and down, willing him to do it, to lose himself. It was like seducing Narcissus.

"Oh God," he moaned. His eyes opened and met hers and were full of mocking self-love as his fist moved faster in his lap. "Look at that face, Gino. She's never even tasted a cock. Doesn't even know what she's missing, but God, how she wants to. She wants to taste mine, doesn't she? She wants to suck my prick, take it between her tits and lick it and worship it. The little slut. The whore. You want it, don't you? Don't you? Tell me you want it, Vanessa. Tell me you want it!"

"Yes," she said breathlessly. "Yes, I want it. I want all of it."

"Pull your cups down," he gasped. "Pull them down and let me see your tits. Hold them up for me. Hold them up for me as I come. I want to come on your fucking tits! I want to...I want...Oh God!"

Vanessa peeled the cups of her bra down and pushed her breasts out like peeled fruit, arching her back to be close to him as Brian's eyes closed and he stiffened in the chair, all his muscles going rigid. He gasped deeply and the room went dead silent for a moment as he held his breath and she saw his stomach tremble with the force of his impending release, the only sound the obscene fleshy slapping of his hand on his cock, and then he exploded—a long, guttural groan accompanied by a soaring jet of semen that arced through the air and hit Vanessa on the cheek—then another, and another, which she caught on her breasts, pressing them together to make a natural funnel to collect his hot discharge.

Brian groaned, his ass arched off the chair as he ejaculated onto Vanessa's proffered flesh, then he shuddered deeply— once, and again—and fell back into the seat, his hips

131

continuing to jerk as the remains of his semen streamed down his cock and his pumping fingers.

She'd been so fixated on his orgasm that she didn't even notice Gino standing next to her already masturbating through his boxers 'til he grabbed her hair and forced her to look at him. He held her eyes with his—a look of contempt, of jealousy perhaps for making Brian come—as he rapidly fisted his short, thick cock and Vanessa stared right back, daring him to do it, daring him to prove he was man enough and then Gino swore and threw his head back and his thick, hot seed splashed onto her breasts as well, his hips jerking in spasmodic release.

He pushed, he jerked, squeezing the last bits of it out and then he let her go, doing his best to walk steadily back to the sofa and sit as if it had all meant nothing to him, but Vanessa noticed his legs shaking.

She remained on her knees, feeling the men's come seeping thickly over her breasts and between them. She hung her head, partly in shame, but partly so the men wouldn't see the look of triumph she wore, of understanding. With her face down, she could sense the overpowering smell of male release.

Brian was the first to recover and with his left hand—the hand he hadn't used—he pulled over a box of tissues and began to clean himself off, carefully wiping off his fingers and paying special attention not to get any semen on his shirt or trousers, then he pushed the box toward Vanessa.

"I think we have a deal then," he said. "Our first show is Wednesday night. A kind of a trunk show. We go on at nine. I'll pick you up at seven, Vanessa. You'll want to get there early, meet the girls, get your hair done."

Vanessa wiped off her breasts with the tissues, remembering the old story of there being nothing better for your complexion. "But won't we have a rehearsal? A run-through?"

"Oh no. No need. It's all very casual. You'll see."

"Well then, I can drive myself."

"No," Brian said, sitting up and pulling up his shorts, "I really like to drive my new girls. Sometimes they get nervous, though there's nothing to be nervous about. Really. Nothing at all."

Chapter Eight

ဆ

"I'm going out to Jessica's, Mom. Going to help her with her calculus and then she's got this movie we're going to watch, so I might be kind of late."

Her mom turned her head from the TV and looked at her and Vanessa was glad Cheryl wasn't there. Cheryl knew all the tricks about getting out of the house and would have seen right through her, but Vanessa's lies were still novel enough to be believed. She was getting good at lying. It didn't even feel wrong anymore, just necessary.

"Did you get your message, dear? Mr. Taylor called and wanted you to call him. He said it was important."

Mr. Taylor had been calling her cell all day to the point that Vanessa had programmed the phone to block his number. "Oh? Did he? Okay. I'll call him as soon as I get to Jessica's. Must be about the shop."

"You want the car, dear?" her mother asked.

"No. I'll walk. Could use the exercise. I've got my cell if you need me."

"Well, Jessica will drive you home, right? I don't want you out at that hour."

"Of course, Mom, sure." She came over and kissed her mother on the head, then grabbed her book bag and slipped out the door, trying to look as normal as possible. It seemed to her that she closed the door unusually hard though.

She wouldn't meet Brian in front of her house, that was for sure, and she pulled up the hood on her sweatshirt as she cut through the alley to the fast food place on the next block. His Lexus was parked all alone at the far end and she sighed.

She'd have to cross the empty space and she didn't want to be seen. She trotted over and climbed inside. He had a Palm Pilot in his lap and was entering some figures. He smiled when he saw her.

"Good. On time. I like that. You ready?"

"I guess so," she said. "Now tell me about this. What's going to happen?"

He pulled out of the lot and headed north. "Nothing special. Just like I said. You'll be modeling lingerie—just putting it on, walking out there, doing your little spin, walking back. Next girl goes out and you change into your next outfit. We start at nine, by eleven, eleven-thirty it's all over, unless you want to stay later."

"Stay later?"

Brian shrugged noncommittally. "Some girls stay later to do some more modeling. A kind of encore thing, understand? There's big money there. Big tips. If you want to make some serious money, you'll consider it."

He swung the car onto the highway and headed out of town.

"How many girls will be there?"

"Tonight? Oh, the usual. This is a regular gig, every Wednesday. Six girls. Well, six models, including yourself, then Angie and Felicia will be there from the lingerie company to help with wardrobe. Aaron and Rio will be there and they'll stick around—they drive the van and help out—and Gino should be there too."

He saw the worried look on her face and added, "Don't worry about it, Vanessa. I run a legitimate business and we have strict guidelines. No one touches you and you don't touch anyone. You don't go anywhere with the clientele while you're on company time. That's our policy and written into our contract. Strictly legitimate. Of course, what you do on your own time is your business. We can't control everything."

"What does that mean?"

135

Brian gave her a dry, knowing look. "It means that our policies apply while you're working for us. When the show ends, you're not officially working for us. That's all it means."

He reached over and turned on the radio and she realized she wasn't supposed to ask any more questions.

He pulled the car off the highway and Vanessa realized they were near the airport, a strip of hotels and motels and bars in an unincorporated area the kids in high school had referred to as the Patch, a place where you could get liquor and supposedly almost anything else. The hotels ended and the road grew rough and then there was a big graveled lot and a squat, ugly blue building with a neon sign that said "Woodies". She was about to comment on the misspelling when she realized that maybe it wasn't an accident. The parking lot was full.

Brian pulled around to the back where some men were unloading boxes from a white van. "The outfits," Brian informed her. "That's Aaron and Rio. They work for me."

He went and greeted the men and Vanessa got out and looked around. A big jet passed overhead with a deafening roar, so close she could see the treads on the tires as it approached the airport. The back door of the club was open and she peered inside at the yellow light. A corridor, a noisy kitchen on one side, some waitresses and busboys rushing around, hauling bins of dishes and trash.

Brian was still talking to the men so Vanessa walked into the club. Besides the chaotic kitchen, there was an office and some storerooms and a big room that must be where they'd change. Cases of beer and hard liquor were stacked against one wall and space had been made for the racks of clothes and some chairs and mirrors. Vanessa glanced at the clothes in their protective plastic bags—a lot of black, a lot of sheer, a lot of shiny. Two girls were putting on makeup and didn't even look up. She walked past them and past some trash bins and then the corridor grew dark and she walked out through some doors and into the bar itself.

Vanessa wasn't that experienced but she knew enough to recognize a strip club when she saw one. The room was dark and cavernous and loud with the sound of rock music, and from where she stood an elaborate bar snaked back and forth providing maximum seating room. Beyond the bar were tables and booths stretching off into the cavernous darkness. There were three brass poles reaching from the bar up to the ceiling and she didn't need to be told what these were for. Racks of spotlights hung from the dark ceiling. There were maybe forty or fifty men inside, some in suits, some in T-shirts and jeans, but the place was just starting to fill up. It smelled like beer and cigarettes and frying oil.

"When we get started," she jumped to find Brian at her elbow, "there'll be stairs right here where we're standing. You'll walk up the stairs, across the bar there and out onto that runway. See where there's no stools? That's ringside, the best seats, and they sell those and we get a cut, so if you want to do a little bump and grind, that's the place to do it. Then you do your pirouette, show some skin and walk back along the other side. There'll be stairs there too, and you go back and change into your next outfit and come out this way again. See? It's simple."

"It's a strip club!" Vanessa said.

Brian gave her a disdainful look. "It's not a strip club. It's a gentlemen's club, honey. This is a lingerie show and these men want to see girls in lingerie. Aaron and Rio will be by the stairs and see that no one gets fresh, but let's not kid ourselves. This is a business, honey, and this is how it's done."

Vanessa looked up at the bar. She supposed she could do it. Just walk along the bar, eyes straight ahead, maybe roll her hips a little. There'd be shouts and catcalls, but the bar was wide enough that no one would grab her and she'd walk the length of the bar and do a spin and then she'd be through the other door and backstage again. She just had to keep her mind a blank.

Brian turned to an Asian girl in jeans and a T-shirt—a very tight T-shirt—who'd come out to look at the crowd. The girl wore a baseball cap on her head and was chewing gum. She seemed very relaxed.

"This is China," he said to Vanessa. "China, Vanna."

"Vanna?" Vanessa looked him.

"Yeah. Your stage name. You want a stage name. Never give out your real name." He turned back to China. "She's the new girl. You get her ready, show her the ropes? You two ought to get along fine. Both college girls. I've got to get the music ready."

China watched Brian leave then raised her eyebrows at Vanessa in a what-can-you-do attitude. "You really are new, huh?" she asked.

"Yes. It's my first show."

"Don't worry about it. It's nothing really. I've been doing it for about three years now, this and dancing. Putting myself through graduate school. Mesoamerican archaeology. You?"

"Uh, mechanical engineering."

"Good for you. You'll make more money than I will in archaeology. My real name's Lauren, by the way." She put out her hand. "Brian made me China. 'China's Vagina.' I guarantee you you'll hear that at least once tonight. Lauren Vu. I'm not even Chinese. Vietnamese."

"Vanessa," she said.

"Come on," Lauren said. "Let's get into the changing room while there's still time."

Vanessa followed Lauren back past the trash cans in something of a daze. The music was loud, the kitchen staff and waitresses and busboys were pushing past and Rio was taking clothes out of boxes and hanging them on racks, knocking into everyone.

Lauren introduced Vanessa to Tracy, a thirtyish blonde with a killer body but a face that wasn't quite good enough, her complexion scarred by acne. There was a brunette named Beth, a Charmaine and a beautiful black girl whose name was Sienna, engaged in some sort of argument with her boyfriend on a cell phone.

It took Lauren about five minutes to put her makeup on, turning herself from a pleasant-looking Asian girl in a baseball cap to an exotic slut, still in a baseball cap, then she turned her seat over to Vanessa and Vanessa got out her makeup. Behind her in the mirror she saw Lauren strip off her jeans, then take off the cap and shake out an amazing mane of jet-black hair that fell almost to her behind. She saw Vanessa looking at her and smiled.

"It's a pain in the ass but the men love it," she said. "Just like these."

She lifted her T-shirt over her head and Vanessa looked at her breasts, big and high and round, and obviously not natural.

"Three grand and that was cheap," Lauren said. "I didn't use that hack Simmonds that Brian uses. This guy was good. I figure I made it back in tips in like three months." She laughed then saw the look of dismay on Vanessa's face.

"Look, Vanessa, you don't have to do this kind of stuff if you don't want. The surgery and all that. Sienna's all natural and she does just fine. It just depends on how much money you want to make. It's a business."

The other girls were changing now, and the room was full of bodies and legs and satin and spandex and hair spray. Vanessa suddenly felt as out of place here as she did in advanced Strength of Materials class dressed in her jeans and flannel shirt, only reversed. Instead of feeling like a girl in a room full of men she felt like a boy in a room full of women.

Lauren came over and helped with her makeup, accentuating her eyes, her cheekbones, the gloss of her lips, giving her a predatory face. She backcombed her hair a bit to give it fullness and sprayed it in a way they'd played with in

139

the salon so that some strands fell in her face, giving her a wanton and slutty look. Lauren squatted down behind her and looked over her shoulder with approval—with something more than approval.

"You ever do girls, Vanessa?" she whispered.

She should have been outraged, but her image was working on her again, her own look of sexual readiness. Both girls were in the underwear and Lauren's face was beautiful. "No," she said, though at the moment she didn't want to shut out the possibility.

"Well, one of the things about this job is that it can turn you off men pretty quick. If you ever want to try…" Lauren smiled at her in the mirror and gave her a soft kiss on the side of the neck that Vanessa felt down in her stomach, then put a glass down on the dressing table. "Try some of this if you start getting nervous."

"I get two hundred for some girl-on-girl," Tracy said, and Vanessa realized she'd been watching them from the background. "It's not bad for four or five minutes of kissing and a little ass-grabbing."

In the mirror Vanessa saw Lauren's eyes meet Tracy's and warn her off, but Vanessa had already heard and the damage was done. Tracy just flipped her hair and walked off.

"Wh-what?" Vanessa blurted out, as her entire predicament was starting to register.

Brian came in, rubbing his hands. "Okay, ladies. Ten minutes to show time. Sienna! Would you get off the damn phone already? You've got ten minutes to get ready! Ten minutes." He walked out.

"What did she mean?" Vanessa asked again, already knowing the answer.

Lauren was slipping into her first outfit—a tight black Chinese dress that buttoned along the collar, so short it barely covered her crotch.

"Honey," she said, stepping into some matching heels. "You don't have to do anything you don't want to do, but most of us make our real money from tips and extras."

"Extras?"

Lauren looked at her and saw that Vanessa really didn't understand. She helped Vanessa adjust her first outfit, a fairly conservative black camisole with a little silk jacket. "Honey, you really are new to this, aren't you? Extras are special modeling sessions, photos, lap dances, whatever else they can get."

"But Brian said—"

"I know what Brian said," Lauren interrupted. "It's against company policy to get personal or touch or be touched, and I'm sure it is. He said the same thing to all of us, but that's just legal bullshit so that he's covered if we're ever busted. The extras are done all on our own. Our own time, our own initiative."

Lauren saw the stunned look on Vanessa's face but there was no time to help soothe her nerves now at this late date. She only had time for the essentials. "Just remember this— never say, 'I'll do this-or-that for so much money', or 'If you want to touch me there, that'll cost you fifty bucks'. Never offer skin for money, nothing like that. That's soliciting. That's prostitution." She yanked on Vanessa's cami to get her attention. The girl looked like she was in shock.

"Always let the john make the proposal," Lauren continued. "Cops aren't allowed to do that. That's entrapment. So if he says, 'I'll give you fifty bucks if you let me lick your tits', then you know you're okay. You can do that. And be very careful of any kind of insertion, baby. They don't go for that here. Use the parking lot or a motel, but I'd stay strictly away from that if I were you. I don't do it. Not just because of the law but because of AIDS, STDs. Just don't do it, and if you do, always make the fucker wear a rubber no matter what you do, remember? Always, got it?"

141

The music suddenly struck up outside—some rock anthem—and lights started sweeping the bar in a bewildering display, as if looking for something. Vanessa stared at Lauren, finally realizing exactly what she had let herself in for, but Lauren was already composing her stage face, making her features blank and pinching her nipples to make them stand up and show through the silk.

Brian's voice cut over the music on the speaker system, talking it up and reminding the patrons that all these fashions were for sale at the booth in front of the bar and that the girls would be available for photos as well at the private session to follow, open to members only. Memberships were on sale but were limited so hurry and sign up now. Then there was something about China modeling a mini playwear wrap in Shantung silk with ivory buttons or something and Lauren turned to her one last time.

"You'll be fine!" she said. "They can't make you do anything you don't want to do, just remember that. Now break a leg!" And then she walked around the corner and out into the blazing white of a spotlight, a big smile on her face. There was a roar of applause.

Aaron leaned against the wall, peeking out into the bar, and after a certain amount of time and after the applause had died down, he took Vanessa by the arm. She heard Brian announce Vanna, fresh from college, as smart as she was pretty, wearing a black silk camisole and matching jacket, and then Aaron pulled her out. "Here you go, honey."

Vanessa stepped into the dark room and saw the stairs leading to the bar. Aaron handed her up, as unsteady as she was in these high, unfamiliar heels and from the top of the wooden bar all she could really see was spotlight. Then she saw the tops of some heads and then the faces of the men seated eagerly at her feet, their drinks in front of them and piles of bills.

Don't look at them! she told herself, and she started her walk. Brian was saying something over the PA, but Vanessa could barely make it out over the thump of the music. Strangely, there wasn't the roaring and catcalling, the hooting and whistling she'd expected. Instead, the men seemed awed into respect as she walked along and that respect excited her.

It was like a dream and a nightmare. It was the fantasy she'd always had, but now it was real and grimy and filled with fear and confusion. Instead of seeing the love and desire in men's eyes, she saw the piteous look of lust and cheap want.

She walked. She walked as she'd seen models walk, one foot in front of the other, letting her hips roll, and then her shoulders, keeping her chest and her head high, looking at nothing, though she could see Brian's shadow out in the audience behind the microphone and an audio mixing board. She could see Gino with him too, leisurely taking pictures, but she ignored them. The bar was wide and she had plenty of room, and she put her shoes down on the polished surface one after the other as the eyes looked up at her. Vanessa felt that sense of power start to come back to her. She was nervous as hell, frightened almost out of her wits, but she felt those men's eyes reaching for her and wanting her. Some she knew wanted to fuck her, but others just wanted to look, maybe touch, maybe just have her recognize them, but she didn't.

She let the little jacket swirl behind her as she made her turn at the end of the bar, and as she walked back, hands were raised at her, hands holding money, but she didn't know what she should do so she walked past them. She made her final turn and then she was at the end of the long bar and Rio was there, waiting to help her down and hustle her into the back.

Vanessa was hurried into the changing room ringing with adrenaline, her heart in her mouth. Someone shoved a drink in her hand and she gulped it down and made a face. She still didn't like liquor. She started stripping off her clothes, putting on the next outfit, and one of the girls said to her, "Why didn't you take the money? They were giving you money!"

"Idiot," Tracy said to the girl, pulling on her nylons. "That was her first pass. Let it go. Make the bastards sweat. See what they offer her next time through."

"It's a good crowd."

"Great crowd."

"Always a good crowd out here, sitting by the bar. Wait'll afterwards!"

"How'd you do? How'd it go?" Lauren asked, running through. She just had time to look into Vanessa's face and squeeze her hand and then she was lining up for her second run in some sort of slashed, see-through harem pants and tiny bra, Aaron shoved his arm through the door to gesture her to come out and out she went.

And that's the way the evening went—impossible chaos in back, then the calm, sultry parade before the patrons' eyes out front. Stockings, corsets, collars, lost shoes, men's hands holding money and drinks, more drinks in back—the adrenaline-fueled moment when she mounted the stairs and felt the eyes on her. Vanessa learned to take the money and fold it into her hand, not like some of the other girls, like Lauren, who spread out the bills she was given and held them like a Chinese fan, or Tracy, who stuffed them into her cleavage or the waist of her panties.

And then there were no more outfits to be modeled. The changing room was a mess, with outfits and stockings and shoes all over the place and the two lingerie reps trying to collect and sort through all the garments and girls gulping drinks and fixing smudged makeup. They huddled in the back, high and excited, all talking at once, 'til Gino came in and said, "Time for your big encore," and Rio started handing out T-shirts with the name of the lingerie company on it.

"Just put it on," Lauren said. "It's part of the show. Leave your stockings, but nothing else. Nothing underneath. No panties."

Vanessa did as she was told and lined up with the other girls in a knot then, to loud applause and excited whistling, they all went out and mounted the bar to make their curtain calls, holding hands like a chorus line. They walked out to the center of the bar — the part that extended out into the crowd near where Brian stood now, holding the microphone, and then, at the sound of his countdown — "Three... Two... One..." the men sitting around the bar let go with a fusillade of liquid — spraying the girls with water from squirt guns, super-soakers, squirt bottles, even seltzer siphons, drenching them, soaking them — their faces, their bodies, their hair, wetting the T-shirts so that they clung to their bodies like transparent tissue, putting everything on display. Vanessa saw Brian standing up with a hose, connected to God-knows-where, spraying the girls and laughing.

There was nothing to do but stand there in front of the crowd and take it, cowering, humiliated, effectively naked and drenched by the outpourings of liquid from the men they'd just entertained. The bartenders laughed and ducked out of the way, the men stood on their stools, aiming their streams at the girls they fancied. Some of the girls, like Lauren and Tracy, had clearly expected it and stood there facing the deluge proudly, but others were too shocked to move. Vanessa had never felt anything like it and she cowered, tried to hide as her T-shirt became transparent, her nipples peaked with cold and her entire body was put on display.

There was applause and laughter, another shower of money — coins this time — thrown as if in contempt, and then they were herded off the stage and into the back as Brian stood on his chair with the microphone and announced above the shouts and whistles, "The show continues upstairs for you Gold Key Members, and if you're not a member, memberships can still be purchased right here, folks."

In the back, the girls were stripping off their soaked T-shirts and drying themselves off. They were swearing and laughing, toweling their hair, kicking off wet shoes. Vanessa hadn't been the only one surprised by the show's big finish and some of the girls were fuming.

"At least can't we take a goddamned shower? Is there a fucking shower in the place? Some asshole threw beer on me and I smell like a brewery!" one girl said.

"There's showers upstairs," Tracy replied. "Save the shower for upstairs. They'll pay good money to watch you shower."

"Upstairs?" Vanessa turned to one of the experienced models she knew as Beth. "We're going upstairs now?"

"Yeah, baby. That's the private club where the high rollers are. That's where the real money's made. Just towel yourself and Gino will give you an outfit. The private modeling's upstairs. That's where they get to examine the goods."

"But what about all that stuff Brian said. No one touches us, we don't touch anyone..."

"Baby, we're not on company time anymore. We're on our own. We're no longer working for Brian Ackerman Productions once we step out of this room."

"Except for the cut he takes," Tracy interjected.

"Off the books," Beth replied, slipping into a dry pair of heels and throwing a robe around her. "Strictly off the books."

Suddenly it dawned on Vanessa what she had gotten herself into—not just modeling, but some sort of B-girl scam or something even worse.

Brian came in with Gino, keeping his immaculate clothes well clear of the models who were still dripping water and shaking out their hair. "We ready, ladies? Ready? The stairs are around back here. Give the clients five minutes to order their drinks and find their seats and then we make our grand entrance. All set, Gino?"

"No," Vanessa said, pushing through the crowd. "I didn't agree to this. I'm not going out there to strip for a bunch of strangers or give lap dances or whatever you do."

146

Some girls looked at her but most of them were getting ready, brushing out their hair or repairing their makeup.

"So you don't want to go?" Brian asked. "Okay. I can't make you, though you're missing some big money, Vanessa. Some really righteous money."

"I don't care. I was hired to model and that's what I've done. And now I'm leaving."

"You'd better call a cab," Gino said over his shoulder. "It's a long ride."

"Just give me my money and I'll take care of the cab," Vanessa said bitterly.

Brian pulled a sheaf of papers out of his jacket pocket and shuffled through them. He selected one and handed it to her and Vanessa stared at it for several moments before she realized what it was—a bill for $4,834, due Brian Ackerman Productions, Ltd.

"I'll apply tonight's pay to what you owe the agency," Brian said, waiting to take the paper from her wet fingers. "If you want cab fare, maybe one of the boys out front will lend it to you."

Vanessa stared at the bill again. Hair styling and consultation: $650. Makeup consultation: $400. Studio time: $3,000… The list went on. She'd even been billed for being driven to this job.

"What is this?" she asked. "You never told me I'd be paying for this!"

"Standard practice," Brian said, pulling the paper from her stunned grip. "Standard contract, Vanessa. You signed it when you signed the photo release forms. Don't tell me you didn't know."

"I certainly didn't! No one ever told me…"

"You owe Brian Ackerman Productions almost five grand, Vanessa. Now you either find some way to pay me that money or you'll be in some serious trouble. We might even have to start selling your publicity shots on the Web, suitably enhanced of course."

"You son of a bitch! You motherfucker...!"

Lauren came up behind her and took her arm. "Don't piss him off," she whispered. "He's not bad to work for and gives you your money, but he and Gino can be real trouble when you mess with them. Didn't you read that contract?"

"No," Vanessa exclaimed. "They just told me they were release forms and standard contracts."

Lauren was about to say something, but then Gino came through handing out costumes to the girls. To Tracy he gave a vinyl cat suit, another girl got a little girl's pinafore and another got a metallic dress that Vanessa recognized as not that different from what Mr. Taylor had her wear at the casino. She almost felt jealous. Gino looked at Vanessa and gave her an exaggerated smile, then searched through the remaining costumes and handed her a hanger dripping with straps and buckles and chains. Vanessa took it and held it up, trying to make out what it was and saw that it was some sort of BDSM outfit—a latex bustier with garters and straps and chains that would cover her breasts. There were cuffs for her wrists and ankles and a leather collar with a long silver leash.

"Here you go, Vanessa," Gino said with a big smile. "You're going to be Tracy's bitch. She'll lead you in on a chain."

"No," she said, already feeling the heat in her cheeks. "No way. I'm not wearing this."

"Just do it!" Lauren hissed, already slipping the bustier around her and pulling up the big zipper. "Just do it and get it over with. So you show some boob, sit in their laps, maybe jerk them off or let them suck your tits or beat off on your ass, and walk out with a fistful of cash. These old farts aren't going to last long anyway and this is where we make our money."

Vanessa saw she had no choice and furiously sat down and started pulling on the black stockings and attaching them to the garters, then Lauren and another girl helped her with the cuffs and anklets as Vanessa stood there in shock. It wasn't just the outrage of what she was going to have to do, but the sudden illicit thrill she felt as the soft leather manacles were tightened over her wrists that alarmed her. The bustier hugged her with that familiar erotic feeling and Lauren tugged up her panties in the back, putting pressure against her crotch. In spite of her humiliation and nervousness, Vanessa felt herself growing aroused. Brian could say what he wanted, but she knew that this time there was going to be touching, that she was going to be on display like a common whore and that she was going to have to do things.

Gino and Brian hustled all the girls together in a group and led them up the back stairs to a big fire door where Brian held his finger to his lips for silence. "We ready?"

Gino knelt down and attached a silver chain between Vanessa's ankles. It was long enough to allow her to walk, but the symbolism was clear. He took her wrists and snapped the cuffs together with a silver clip then took the leash and handed it to Tracy. He stopped just briefly to look into Vanessa's eyes, daring her to say anything, then handed her a card with a number on it—number four. All the girls had numbers.

"Hold them where they can see them," Brian said, then he shoved open the door and led the girls inside.

This wasn't the same raucous scene it had been below. There was no stage, no bar to separate them from the audience, just a clear spot on the floor with bright spotlights trained upon it that made seeing anything outside the cone of light very difficult. Surrounding the empty space were tables and Vanessa could just make out the tops of men's heads through the glare.

A man from the bar stood in the middle of the floor with the obsequious manners of an MC. "Welcome to the special showing," he said. "Those of you who've been here before know how it works. For our new patrons, we like to work this as an auction. We know you've all been impressed with our collection and would like to get a closer look at these exciting fashions, so to make things fair, we'll allow you to bid on the rights to a private showing. Now, our first model is Carrie, wearing this fetching harem playsuit. What am I bid for the chance to have a closer look at Carrie's harem outfit?"

Voices called out numbers. Fifty dollars, a hundred dollars, a hundred and fifty. Carrie was a pro and knew how to pose, strutting around in the spotlight and using her number card to lift her breasts suggestively and the bidding soared.

Vanessa watched, horrified. Her outfit had no top, just rows of cold silver chains that draped across her breasts and made her nipples embarrassingly erect, and there was no denying that having her hands bound excited her. She stood there among the girls like a slave at auction and Tracy had to keep on jerking her leash and whispering, "Keep your head up! They want to see your face!"

Carrie went for three hundred dollars and there was a burst of laughter as she dropped her number and strutted over to the man who'd bought her. Vanessa's eyes had adjusted enough to the dark now that she could see Carrie sit in the man's lap and put her arms around his neck and the man untying the top of her outfit with obvious greed.

The bidding continued. Beth went next for four hundred and then Lauren, who knew how to work the crowd too, walking out to the center of the spotlight and running a finger over her breasts and down to her crotch as the bidding climbed into a raucous shouting match. Vanessa didn't even hear the price because the MC came over and took her leash from Tracy and marched her out into the middle of the light.

The room grew still. Vanessa kept her hands up against her breasts but the man pushed them down so her nipples could be seen poking through the cascade of chains. All those men out there, she thought. All those cocks hard for me, all those eyes on me. How far she'd come from her game in her bedroom—how far and how close to realize her dream and how different it was in reality. Her face colored. Her heart was in her throat.

They'd just make her sit on their laps, Lauren had said. Maybe they'd suck her breasts or make her touch herself. Maybe she'd have to turn around and let them ejaculate on her behind, or her chest, or maybe she'd have to masturbate them herself, using her hands on them.

"Two hundred dollars!" someone called out, and Vanessa felt like she was going to faint.

"Two-fifty!" called another.

And then, from the back, "Two thousand dollars!"

The room went dead. Heads turned.

The MC shielded his eyes with his hand and peered into the darkness, trying to see who would make such an outrageous bid.

"Did I hear two thousand dollars?"

"Two thousand dollars," the voice repeated, and Vanessa's heart flipped in her chest. She knew that voice. Rob Taylor. She choked back a sob.

"We only take cash here, friend," the MC said.

"I know that."

He was approaching the front now, a coat thrown over his shoulder, and Vanessa could make out his shape, the way he walked. It was Rob. There was no doubt.

"I know that and I've got your money right here."

Rob reached into his pocket and handed two stacks of bills to the surprised MC. Gino, watching suspiciously from the shadows along the wall, started forward but Brian put a hand on his arm and held him back, his eyes fixed on the transaction before him. The MC hefted the bundles of bills and riffled through them, then darted a nervous glance over at Brian, his face a sickly blend of suspicion and greed. Brian nodded slowly and the MC stuffed the money into his pocket and quickly regained his wits. "Any other bids?" he called out. "Two thousand dollars! Going once... Going twice..."

There were no other bids.

Rob walked over to where Vanessa stood in the spotlight and the room was absolutely still. He took the leash in his hand as if it were something precious and gave a slight tug and Vanessa, despite her shock and humiliation, felt the tug and took a step toward him. There was something so right and perfect about the way he held the leash that tears formed in her eyes.

Rob took his coat and draped it over her shoulders and Vanessa pulled it close, wrapping herself in its warmth and hiding herself in it. For her, the show was over, and Rob took her arm and led her back past the other girls toward the fire door in back, walking slowly because of the chains still on her ankles. Vanessa kept her eyes down but she heard the girls' whispers of goodbye and good luck and Tracy actually came over and kissed her, with tears in her eyes.

Rob shoved open the fire door and they stepped out into the corridor. He put his hands on Vanessa's shoulders and stood her against the wall, then looked into her eyes to make sure she was all right. Satisfied, he knelt at her feet and unclipped the chain from her ankles.

He stood up, wrapping the silver chain around his left fist. "Stick your head through that door and get your friend Brian to come out here."

"Rob, he's not my friend. It was all a mistake—"

"I know damn well who he is," Rob said. "Just do it."

She'd never seen a look in his eyes like that—hot, like when he wanted her, but cold and dangerous as well, and she knew there was no reasoning with him. She pushed open the heavy door and caught Brian's eye easily enough. He was already looking their way. He grinned when he saw her and came walking over, telling Gino to stay put with a hand gesture.

As soon as Brian came through the fire door Rob kicked it closed behind him and backed him up against the wall, his fury clearly catching Brian by surprise.

"Look, friend," Brian said, raising his hands defensively. "What you just did is a private transaction between you and Vanna here and has nothing to do with Brian Ackerman Productions. We have a strict policy against—"

Rob hit him in the stomach so hard that Brian's feet left the floor and spittle flew from his mouth. He fell back against the wall and then crumpled to the concrete, gasping for breath, his face the color of boiled beets.

Rob bent down over him. "Listen, motherfucker. You come near this girl again, or try to enforce any of your bullshit contracts, and I'll fix it so no one will ever look at the front of your head again without wanting to puke. Understand? I know you, Ackerman. I know the kind of slime you are."

Brian couldn't breathe to answer, but Rob waited patiently until he was able to nod his head, then he suddenly grabbed Brian's arm and pulled it and put the heel of his boot on Brian's fingers and stood up, threatening to bring his weight down on Ackerman's hand with just a step.

"No!" Brian gasped. "Not my hands! Not my hands!"

Rob stood poised there with his boot above Brian's hand, then relaxed and kicked his hand aside as if it were trash. He stood up and put his arm around Vanessa and led her down the stairs, stopping halfway to look back up to where Ackerman lay groaning on the dirty cement.

"And by the way—nice suit."

Chapter Nine

ᏇᎧ

She didn't care that people stared at her as they walked into the hotel, her stockings and heels showing beneath an oversized man's raincoat and her hair still damp from her earlier dousing. She didn't care that she still wore the collar and leash they'd put on her in the club or that her elaborate makeup was smeared with tears. It was raining out and that would explain both the coat and her bedraggled appearance, but mostly she just didn't care. She just kept her face down and held his coat closed around her neck so no one would see and let him lead her past the desk and across the lobby and into the elevator. They hadn't spoken two words since he drove her away from the club. She'd tried, but she didn't know where to start and Rob didn't look like he needed any answers.

Another couple got on the elevator with them but one look at Vanessa with her head down and Rob's menacing silence covering her like a protective cloak and the man and woman discreetly fixed their eyes on the floor indicator and exited quickly and without a word.

On the seventh floor Rob led her off the elevator and down the hallway to a room and it was then, when he ushered her inside and turned on the bedside light and she saw a pair of jeans and a sweater lying on the bed waiting for her that she broke down — the shame, the humiliation, his goodness all too much for her. He came up to her and took her in his arms and she grabbed onto him as if she were drowning, tears streaming down her face, hiding herself in his body.

"Oh God, Rob!"

He held her tight and let her cry, let her sob as rain spattered against the windows and far below cars streamed slowly on the expressway. She wanted to make herself small, so small she'd disappear into his arms and never be seen again, but Rob just held her, keeping her there and making her face her grief. He wouldn't let her disappear and wouldn't let her go 'til at last her tears exhausted themselves. And still he was holding her and she realized at last that he was holding her for his own comfort as well as her own.

He let go of her carefully, as if there was still a chance she might fall apart, then sat down in one of the chairs. Vanessa missed the feel of his body so much that she was ready to do anything to feel him against her again—sex, affection, whatever he wanted. The feel of the intimate lingerie she wore, the ambience of the anonymous hotel room and the sight of him sitting in the chair brought back the memories of all the nights they had spent like this, and despite herself she felt herself ready for his touch. Then she realized with disappointment that he hadn't brought her here for sex.

He poured them two drinks from an open bottle and handed her one, and Vanessa remembered that first night in her kitchen, trying to drink the whiskey to make herself feel wicked. The tears almost started again. She said, "You know I don't drink."

He smiled. "Learn."

She took a sip and felt the searing heat, not as bad as she'd remembered from before, or maybe she just needed it now. She took another drink and felt the liquor spread warmth through her body. Beneath the raincoat she still wore her outfit and the chains were cold against her naked breasts. The whiskey warmed her up.

"I tried to warn you about Ackerman," Rob said. "But you weren't answering your cell. I tried to check around to find out who he was, but no one in the business knew him. I know a model who knows everyone though and she knew him. She knew McCall too and all about their business. She filled me in."

"But how'd you find me?"

"Vanessa, they do those shows three, four times a week. That's his business—he even advertises in the paper. Lingerie shows, live models, bring your camera. Sometimes they're more respectable than they are out at Woodies, but they're never good. I knew you were going to get mauled. He's a pimp, Vanessa. Brian Ackerman is a pimp."

His words were so certain and so final that Vanessa felt her hands start to tremble. If Ackerman was a pimp, she knew what that made her. She put the glass down and clutched the coat closed as if that could protect her. Rob poured her some more whiskey and handed it back to her and suddenly she had to sit down. She sat on the bed as if her legs wouldn't hold her up anymore.

"But the money, the contracts," she said. "I signed them. I owe him like five thousand dollars."

"Fuck him," Rob said. "No one's going to honor his contracts and he knows it. That's all bullshit, Vanessa, all of it, an old scam they use with girls who want to be models or actresses. 'Be a model. Come on down for some free promo pictures.' Then you show up and sign some forms and suddenly you owe them two, three thousand dollars and they scare you into paying.

"Or they get it out of you some other way," he added.

She looked up at him and he said, "It's a con, Vanessa. Been around for years. You were conned."

"But your money—"

He smiled bitterly. "That was real enough. I wanted to get you out of there and money's the only thing these people understand. I didn't want to get into some bidding war with one of those sleazebags over you. Just hit them with some cash and get out of there."

He took a sip of his drink and smiled at her. "Think I went too high?"

She was too upset to see the joke. "How am I ever going to pay you back, Mr. Taylor? I already owe you so much."

He smiled to himself at the way she shifted to "Mr. Taylor" when the talk turned to money. She looked so young sitting there, worried and on edge, like a little girl caught playing with her mother's makeup. For a moment it was hard to recognize in her the face he so often saw, the mature, sexual young woman.

He looked at her and said, "Don't worry about it. It's a gift to you, Vanessa. I got you into this jam and so it's only fair I get you out. If I hadn't taken you to that casino and done what I did with you, if I hadn't made you play these games with me, and if that first night had never happened…"

"Oh no, Rob! Don't talk like that. It wasn't just you."

Their eyes met and he realized that perhaps now she was older than he thought. Perhaps she'd been older than he thought all along.

"Okay then," he said. "I'll just add it to your student loans and you'll pay me back when you get your degree and start making money. And you will be making money, Vanessa, right? Because you're still going to be one of the best mechanical engineers to ever come out of that university. You know that, don't you?"

Vanessa sat up with a start. "Oh my God! My books! I left them at that club!"

"They're in my trunk," he said. He smiled at her. "I wouldn't let you forget your books."

She felt her eyes fill with tears again. She looked down at the jeans lying on the bed, the tags still on them. She didn't even have to look to know they'd be exactly her size. The sweater was exactly the kind of thing she'd wear in her student persona too. There was a shoebox on the floor too — athletic shoes, her brand. He had thought of everything.

She drained her drink to keep from crying again. She'd been such an idiot and such a fool and yet she couldn't control the things she felt now. It was so strangely familiar. Sitting there with him in that hotel room, her slutty attire covered only by his coat, the rain falling on the windows, the man who had done so much to her and brought such wickedness into her life and such pleasure and was even now still watching out for her. If she offered herself now, would he still want her? She felt like it was the only thing she had to give and yet even as she thought it, she realized that things had changed between them and would never be the same. He would never use her again as he'd used her before, if indeed he'd used her at all.

She stood up and walked to the window and pressed her forehead against the glass. She could see him in the reflection of the dark glass, watching her carefully, concerned.

"Then what happens now?" she asked, almost hopefully.

"Now? Now I'd suggest you take a shower and get dressed and I'll take you home."

"That's all?"

He nodded.

"Rob—"

He looked at her and his face got serious. "Vanessa. There's something between us, something serious, though God knows I've done my best to screw it up. Don't laugh at me if I tell you it's love, because that's what it is for me and I know it in my heart. In all this playing we've done and dressing you up and making you into one person or another, you were always Vanessa underneath and I've fallen in love with you.

"But that doesn't mean it's right," he went on, "or that it's good for us. For you especially… You have your future in front of you and growing to do. You still have to find out who you are, who the real Vanessa is. Because of that—for your own good—I think this should be the last time we meet like this. No more games. I won't force you to do anything anymore."

"But you weren't alone," she said. "I mean, you never made me do anything I really didn't want to do."

158

He put down his drink and stood up, came to her and squatted down in front of her. He took her face in his hands and looked into her eyes and she saw into his eyes as well.

"Vanessa," he said.

He closed his eyes and kissed her on the cheek. He kissed her forehead and then on the other cheek. His lips lingered and Vanessa could tell a goodbye kiss when she felt it. He stood up and turned away so she wouldn't see his face.

"Go shower and get dressed and we'll get out of here," he said. "It's over. I can't do this to you anymore."

He stood with his back to her and Vanessa let the coat slip from her shoulders as she'd done so many times before with so many outfits, revealing herself, but this time he wouldn't look and she stood there alone in her outfit. She could see her reflection in the window glass—the stockings, the tight bustier, the collar and leash—and his reflection as well, his back turned to her. Beyond their reflections the cars were still streaming on the expressway, people coming and going, lives being lived or lost.

She turned and went into the bathroom and closed the door. It was quiet in there and private and warm and Vanessa was suddenly exhausted, physically and emotionally. She closed her eyes and leaned against the door, hugging herself, then looked down at her outfit—the corset and nylons, the silver leash still hanging from the collar around her neck. She thought of Lauren and Tracy and Beth and the other girls, what they must be doing right now, when the private show would be in full swing. She tried to imagine the feel of a stranger's hands on her body, a stranger's eyes on her nakedness, and wondered if she could ever treat it as a game like Lauren had suggested. Then she thought of Rob sitting on the other side of the door, waiting for her. She remembered the first time he'd ever touched her and how even then he hadn't felt like a stranger. She thought of the things he'd done to her, the things he'd made her do—the things he'd made her feel. So this is where it ended.

She undressed with a strange reluctance, feeling the fabric pull almost reluctantly away from her skin. There wasn't much to take off—the cuffs and anklets, her shoes, the stockings and corset and panties. She left the collar for last and turned to look at herself in the mirror, her makeup streaked and running, her hair a bedraggled mess. She picked up the chain and let it slide through her fingers. The cold, sensual hardness of the shiny metal was still exciting to her. It made her shiver. After all that had happened, it still excited her.

She remembered that there were two reasons you kept a pet on a leash—to control it and to keep it safe. She removed the collar and turned on the shower.

She got into the shower and stood under the hot spray, letting it wash over her back, then she took a washcloth and held it in the spray, unwrapped one of the small, cheap bars of hotel soap and stopped. All the places he'd taken her to, whether just at his house or to a hotel or motel, he always had her wash with a special soap he brought with him. He didn't want her to use commercial soap. He said it would ruin her skin.

"Rob," she called. "Could you please come in here?"

The door was thin and he heard her easily. He knocked. "Vanessa? Are you okay? What's wrong?"

"Could you come in please? I need some help."

She saw the door open and Rob stepped into the steamy room, closing it behind him. He slid back the frosted glass shower door and looked at her with concern. Vanessa stood there completely nude, her hands clasped together between her breasts, holding the washcloth and the cheap bar of soap, water streaming down her hair and over her face and body.

"My makeup," she said with feigned helplessness. "Can you help me?"

Her call had alarmed him and when he saw that's all she wanted he was irritated. He was about to tell her she knew perfectly well how to wash her makeup off but then he looked at her, one knee cocked demurely over the other to hide her privates, dripping with water like a little girl or like a statue in a fountain, looking up at him through the strands of wet hair. He smiled.

"Here," he said, and he took the cloth and the soap from her. "I forgot to bring my soap. This will have to do. Hold still."

He soaped the rag and gently wiped the powder and mascara from her face as if she were a child, telling her to close her eyes and working carefully over her eyebrows, her eyes, her cheeks, brushing the cloth at her lips as she stood there dripping with water. He did her neck too and watched the water streaming off her breasts and running from her nipples, down the soft plain of her belly.

His sleeves got wet and he stopped and took off his shirt, then rinsed out the cloth and re-soaped it and went over her face again 'til her natural skin was shining through, glowing slightly from the rubbing.

"Rinse off," he told her, and Vanessa turned her face to the spray and let the water wash the soap off her face as he wrung out the cloth.

"Here too," she said, indicating her nipples. "I rouged them for the show."

Rob looked at her and she stared back at him, her hands on her breasts. The front of his pants were spattered with spray from the shower.

He kicked off his shoes and took off his T-shirt, unbuckled his belt and slid his trousers and shorts down off his legs, then pulled off his socks and stepped into the shower, leaving his clothes in a mess on the floor. He pulled the sliding door closed.

Vanessa leaned back against the tile wall and closed her eyes, her hands at her sides, and Rob soaped the rag once again and stopped, staring at her, struck again by her natural beauty. Neither of them had to look to know that he was erect, the hot water streaming over him now as well.

He dropped the cloth and took the soap in his hand and ran it all over her body, over her breasts and her belly and her thighs, turning her around to do her back and her shoulders and her behind, even running his hand between her buttocks, then he turned her to face him again. Her eyes met his as he closed his hands on her breasts then she closed them at the exquisite sensation of her slippery skin sliding through his fingers. Vanessa could hear his breathing increase above the sound of the water as her stiff nipples slid against his palms. He put her hands on his arms and tilted her head back for his kiss.

She didn't have long to wait. His kiss was hard, possessive and almost frantic as he grabbed her ass in one hand and pressed her feverishly against him. She felt the impossibly hard stalk of his erection slide up her soapy belly and she opened her mouth for him, inviting his tongue as the water beat down upon them both, dripping from one body to another, running down their hair and their faces and their fused lips, puddling where her breasts were flattened against his chest.

"Oh God Vanessa! I can't let you go! I just can't!"

"No," she said, "No. I don't want you to. Ever."

She reached for his face and brought his lips to hers again and feasted on them, licking them and sucking them, taking his lip between her teeth and biting him, leaning back so she could rub her nipples against his hairy chest and press her sex against his rigid staff.

Rob reached up and took the hand piece down from the shower and Vanessa had to make room so he could rinse her off, wash all the soap and suds from her skin, then turn her around and do the same 'til she was squeaky clean. He held her buttocks apart and played the water between her cheeks, then adjusted the spray to pulse and aimed it up between her legs, playing the throbbing jets of warm water against the petals of her sex.

"Oh God! Rob! Rob!"

He leaned against her now, his cock slipping between her buttocks, and held her labia apart with one hand as he played the pulsing spray against her pussy, and Vanessa pressed her cheek to the tile walls and clawed at them with her nails, as if she could escape the maddening pleasure.

She was on fire. The show, the danger and humiliation, the lewd excitement of being put on display like that and now the emotional devastation of almost losing him all combined to make her ache for his touch, to be taken and used by him as he always did when they were together. She wanted to be his again. She wanted it with all her body and soul.

"Ohhhh!" she moaned as the spray pushed her to the edge of orgasm. Her legs were spread—she couldn't help it—and her hips twitched convulsively against the wickedly arousing spray. "Take me to bed, Rob! Please! I can't stand it!"

He clumsily fit the hand piece back into the holder so that the water beat down on them again and then he pushed her shoulders back against the wall so that her hips were cocked out at him.

"Right here," he said. "Just like this. Can you stand?"

"Yes I—"

"Hold onto the towel rack."

He lifted her right leg in his hand, lifted her knee up and she felt the head of his cock slide wetly against her eager flesh, searching for her. She reached down to help him find his goal but by bending his knees he found it himself and all she could do was throw her head back and moan as he entered her right there in the shower, the water streaming over their bodies.

"Oh God!" he sobbed, wrapping his free arm around her. "Oh my God Vanessa!"

She tried to move. She tried to give back to him, but poised on one leg with her other thigh in his hand, all she could do was stand there and let him take her, battering into her with all his need and anguish and desperate longing, fucking her like a machine. She held onto his broad shoulders with all her strength and let him take what he needed, shocked as she felt her own orgasm already blooming, unfolding like a flower within her and reaching for him, offering him everything.

"Oh Rob, hold me! Hold me! I'm going to…going to…"

And then it burst over her like a delicious wave of obliterating pleasure, even as she felt him thrust up hard into her and throb, pulse inside her and fill her with a heat hotter than the water that beat down upon them like cleansing rain.

* * * * *

She awoke naked in bed on her tummy to the feel of him dragging the hair from the back of her neck and brushing his lips against the back of her neck and she smiled without opening her eyes. She knew where she was, and she knew who she was with, and she didn't have to look at anything.

He hummed, not quite ready to wake up, and felt the bed creak as he moved on top of her and settled his weight cautiously onto her back. She was shocked when she felt him touching her, because he was already incredibly hard. How long had he been lying there watching her and wanting her? Then she was even more shocked to realize that she was already wet and ready for him. He took a pillow from the head of the bed and slipped it under her hips to raise her up and she lifted her hips to make it easier for him.

He entered her smoothly, effortlessly and with a cautious tenderness that made her smile, a smile that quickly turned to a moan of pleasure as he kept on going, kept on pushing, 'til he filled her completely and she gripped the pillow in her hands as if it were his body.

"What are we going to tell my mother?" she asked as he slowly began to move on top of her.

With his lips against her neck she felt his soft breath of laughter. "Why bring that up now?" he asked. "We'll think of something. You work for me. We fell in love. Stranger things have happened. I believe when she realizes how deep our feelings are for each other she will come around."

Vanessa closed her eyes. He felt so good, so right, touching her in spots she didn't even know she had. He was such an expert with her, as if she was made for him.

She raised her bottom to take him deeper and sighed as he took advantage of her offer. His hands were planted on the mattress on either side of her shoulders and Vanessa gripped his wrists to hold on. His wrists were like steel. He was so strong.

"But what will she think of me now? Her good little girl?"

He stopped, and she felt his lips on her cheek and her ear.

"You worry too much what people think of you, darling," he said softly. "You just be who you are and don't worry about what other people think."

And with that she smiled.

She worked her knees beneath her and wiggled until she'd lifted her behind to him, spread her knees and gave him everything he wanted. Everything she had and everything she was.

Also by Elliot Mabeuse

ဢ

E-Books:

Helene Blackmailed

Overcoming Abigail

The Experiment

Print Books:

Overcoming Abigail

About the Author

ဢ

Elliot Mabeuse is an award-winning author, critic, and porn theorist whose erotic explorations combine depth and insight with a singularly passionate intensity. His interest in the emotional and transformative power of sex gives his writing a unique flavor, and results in works of literate erotica that are sensual, humane, and deeply satisfying.

Retired from the chemical laboratory now, Doctor Mabeuse lives in Chicago where he pursues his interests in the transcendent powers of sexuality, religion, and the riddles of biochemistry.

Elliot welcomes comments from readers. You can find his website and email address on his author bio page at www.ellorascave.com.

Tell Us What You Think

We appreciate hearing reader opinions about our books. You can email us at Comments@EllorasCave.com.

Why an electronic book?

We live in the Information Age — an exciting time in the history of human civilization, in which technology rules supreme and continues to progress in leaps and bounds every minute of every day. For a multitude of reasons, more and more avid literary fans are opting to purchase e-books instead of paper books. The question from those not yet initiated into the world of electronic reading is simply: *Why?*

1. *Price.* An electronic title at Ellora's Cave Publishing and Cerridwen Press runs anywhere from 40% to 75% less than the cover price of the exact same title in paperback format. Why? Basic mathematics and cost. It is less expensive to publish an e-book (no paper and printing, no warehousing and shipping) than it is to publish a paperback, so the savings are passed along to the consumer.

2. *Space.* Running out of room in your house for your books? That is one worry you will never have with electronic books. For a low one-time cost, you can purchase a handheld device specifically designed for e-reading. Many e-readers have large, convenient screens for viewing. Better yet, hundreds of titles can be stored within your new library — on a single microchip. There are a variety of e-readers from different manufacturers. You can also read e-books on your PC or laptop computer. (Please note that Ellora's Cave does not endorse any specific brands.

You can check our websites at www.ellorascave.com or www.cerridwenpress.com for information we make available to new consumers.)

3. *Mobility.* Because your new e-library consists of only a microchip within a small, easily transportable e-reader, your entire cache of books can be taken with you wherever you go.

4. *Personal Viewing Preferences.* Are the words you are currently reading too small? Too large? Too... ANNOYING? Paperback books cannot be modified according to personal preferences, but e-books can.

5. *Instant Gratification.* Is it the middle of the night and all the bookstores near you are closed? Are you tired of waiting days, sometimes weeks, for bookstores to ship the novels you bought? Ellora's Cave Publishing sells instantaneous downloads twenty-four hours a day, seven days a week, every day of the year. Our webstore is never closed. Our e-book delivery system is 100% automated, meaning your order is filled as soon as you pay for it.

Those are a few of the top reasons why electronic books are replacing paperbacks for many avid readers.

As always, Ellora's Cave and Cerridwen Press welcome your questions and comments. We invite you to email us at Comments@ellorascave.com or write to us directly at Ellora's Cave Publishing Inc., 1056 Home Avenue, Akron, OH 44310-3502.

errídwen, the Celtic Goddess
of wisdom, was the muse who
brought inspiration to storytellers and those in the creative arts.
Cerridwen Press encompasses the best
and most innovative stories in all
genres of today's fiction. Visit our site
and discover the newest titles by
talented authors who still get inspired -
much like the ancient storytellers did,
once upon a time.

1515164R0

Printed in Great Britain by
Amazon.co.uk, Ltd.,
Marston Gate.